TRAPPED WITH THE WOODSMAN

WOODSMAN SERIES BOOK 3

M. S. PARKER

BELMONTE PUBLISHING, LLC

Copyright © 2018 Belmonte Publishing LLC

Published by Belmonte Publishing LLC

WOODSMAN SERIES

Thank you so much for reading *Trapped with the Woodsman*, a **stand-alone** book in my Woodsman series.

If you'd like to read them all, you should read them in the following order as some characters appear in all books:

1. Rescued by the Woodsman
2. Unbreak the Woodsman
3. Trapped with the Woodsman

ONE
LEXI

THROUGH THE OPEN WINDOW, THE SOUND OF THE RAIN — and the scent of it — drifted into my room.

Cool air danced across my overheated flesh as hungry fingers slid between my thighs. I closed my eyes at the sensation, biting my lip as I realized how wet I was, how hungry.

How empty.

A shiver broke out over my entire body as expert fingers caressed me, pushing inside my cunt before slowly withdrawing and starting the whole process all over again.

But it wasn't enough.

Rolling onto my belly, I wiggled around, and soon, a thick, heavy cock filled me.

I moved against it, riding the hard ridge as I closed my eyes and worked myself closer to climax. Face pressed into the pillow, I moved harder, faster.

"That's it..." A low groan filled the air. "Harder. Faster."

I moved furiously as the low, tugging warmth hit my belly, an echo of the orgasm that raced ever closer to me.

A crack of thunder punched through the air just outside my window, followed by a flash of lightning that lit my room. I turned my head at the last second, catching just the vaguest glimpse in the mirror's reflection. I could just barely make out what was happening on the bed. I saw me, on my knees, ass up in the air.

Then it was dark again, and my lashes once more fluttered shut.

The wet, frenzied sounds of the cock driving into me were suddenly drowned out by the sound of rain as the skies opened up and released a downpour that made the rain from moments ago seem non-existent. The primal feel of the storm filled the room, an echo of the need burning in me.

My knees shook as I became more frenzied, desperate to climax.

My nipples were hard, aching points, and I shifted again, this time lying on my back, thighs splayed wide as the cock hammered into me. With my free hand, I toyed with one nipple then the other.

There was another rough, hungry groan, and I opened my eyes wide, staring upward as another crack of thunder was followed by the white-hot flicker of lightning.

I slid my hand down my stomach until I was stroking my clitoris. With a hungry moan, I rocked my hips upward, driving the cock deeper into me while strumming my fingers over my clit.

Sweat slicked over skin gone flushed with urgency.

My fingers moved quicker, almost frantic now, and I cried out, shoving upward with my lower body as the cock drilled into me.

The sounds of sex and need filled the air, flooding my senses.

The scent of rain and musky arousal perfumed the air.

My belly went hot and tight as I chased my orgasm.

Then I was coming, and that low, hungry moan echoed around me once more.

Outside, another crack of thunder tore through the torrential night skies, and I turned my head, seeking out the window this time rather than the mirror that hung on my closet door.

Nothing cleared a self-induced, post-coital glow like acknowledging the fact that it had, indeed, been self-induced. I preferred to pretend that some sexy piece of man-art had brought me to orgasm.

Of course, *that* hadn't happened in so many years, I was surprised I hadn't forgotten what sex is.

THIRTY MINUTES LATER, I sat curled up in an armchair in my living room, the gas fireplace I'd bought for the place giving off a comfortably warm glow. It wasn't anywhere near as good as a real fireplace, but it was good enough for me.

For now, at least.

A book sat open in my lap, and I stared out the night-dark windows as rain continued to pour down.

I lived in Estes Park, where we'd been going through a dry spell. This thunderstorm was unusual this time of year, but the weather hadn't exactly been normal around here for a while. Not as much snow fell, and now we were in the middle of a spring thunderstorm that had been going on for over an hour.

It would make work fun tomorrow.

There were almost always those who didn't pay attention to the warnings or use their common sense while visiting the Rocky Mountain National Park. As a park ranger, it was my job to see to their safety.

If I was smart, I'd be in bed already, resting up for the day to come. Instead, I held a high-ball glass with two fingers of whiskey and a book by one of my favorite authors in my lap.

Dragging my attention away from the storm's display, I focused on the book and soon fell into the story.

Nearly an hour later, my whiskey was gone, and my eyes were gritty with fatigue. I was also wishing I'd held off on my earlier masturbation party until I was done reading for the night.

The author was one known for the exploits that her various couples engaged in, and I might have kept on reading, except it was getting harder to keep my eyes open.

I left the book on the table and rose, moving into the kitchen. It was a large area with windows that faced out over a view of the Rockies. I loved spending the day in here cooking or baking, but I rarely indulged. I had the only mouth that needed to be fed in my home, and I could only eat so many cookies before I felt guilty and forced myself to run an extra mile the next morning.

At the large double-sided sink, I rinsed out the glass, then filled it again, drinking a bit of water before rinsing the glass out once more. After placing it in the drying rack, I padded through the empty house, back to my bedroom.

The sheets and comforter were mussed from my earlier exploits, and I went about tidying up the bed. I could never sleep unless the bed was neatly made when I slid in under the sheets.

Once that task was done, I moved over to the window and stared outside. Thanks to the overhang provided by the back porch, I didn't have to worry about water getting inside during the storm, and I breathed in the chilly air. If it wasn't for the warm front that was moving through, we'd probably be caught up in a snowstorm. The weather forecast hadn't entirely ruled it out, either. Although tomorrow was supposed to be almost mild, they were calling for more precipitation and colder weather that would move in tomorrow night.

Thunder rumbled almost constantly overhead, and the lightning continually lit up the sky.

After watching the tumultuous display for a few more minutes, I pulled the window pane down until it was open only an inch.

In the bathroom, I combed my hair and brushed my teeth, then slipped out of the lounge pants I'd pulled on after my shower. Clad in a tank and panties, I climbed into bed, my mind already hazed and cloudy.

Sleep didn't come as easily as I would have thought, though. A fine tension seemed to hum inside me, one that hadn't been completely relieved by my earlier self-play session.

It had been entirely too long since I'd been with a man. Idly, I thought about swinging by one of the bars in town and trying to find somebody to hook up with, but even as I considered it, I brushed the idea off. Tourist season hadn't really started, and I had no desire to try to find one of the locals.

There wasn't a shortage of decent-looking guys in the small town, but I just wasn't all that keen to hook up with somebody who lived here full time. It was too…complicated.

I very much preferred to limit the complications in my life.

I made the decision back in college that my career would come before anything else in life, especially with something as messy as a relationship. After growing up in a home where my mother only barely tolerated me, I wasn't all that sure I was cut out for anything beyond the physical anyway.

TWO
ROMAN

Smooth, full lips slid down my chest.

I closed my eyes, curving my hand around the back of her neck. As she slid lower, she freed the button of my jeans, then dragged the zipper down, never once taking her mouth from my skin.

I groaned as she took me into her mouth, sucking on me until I hit the back of her throat. Fisting my hand in her hair, I dragged her back until just the head of my cock was between her lips, then I urged her back down. Once more, she all but swallowed my cock.

Sweat beaded along my skin as I began to rock up against her mouth, urging her to take me harder and faster.

Her nails raked down my thighs, then moved between my legs to cup my balls in her palm. She pulled away, then lowered her mouth until she could scrape her teeth along the sensitive skin of my sac.

Somewhere off in the distance, my phone rang.

The fantasy shattered around me, just like that.

But my cock was still hard and aching, so ignoring the phone, I once more began stroking myself, my hand pumping up and down with quick, rough movements.

The phone rang again, but I only dimly heard it, focused on the rhythmic pulls of my hand.

Gritting my teeth together, I arched my back.

The orgasm rushed closer, and with a long growl I climaxed; my cum splattering across my belly, trickling down as I continued to fist my cock.

Finally, after one last pump, I let go of my dick. My hand fell to my belly, slick with semen.

For a few more minutes, I lay there, taking a reprieve from the constant noise that almost always battered my mind. Rarely were my thoughts this quiet, and I breathed out a slow, relaxed breath.

I'd been into town earlier and bumped into a woman I'd known for years. We talked for a few minutes, and she ended the conversation with a stroke of her finger across my jaw, the tip brushing along the scar that started at my right ear and ran down vertically along the side of my neck. That scar, along with several others, was among the lingering marks of my years spent in the army. Most of them had all been received in one night.

As Marina smiled up at me, her eyes had gone dark. "Look me up any time you're feeling…lonely," she'd said.

Although I had little interest in Marina – even sexually – it had been a long time since I'd been between a woman's thighs, and that smug little smile of hers had given me ideas.

It had given me a hard-on.

I hadn't taken her up on the offer, but my libido woke up with a vengeance.

Outside the house, I could hear thunder rumble ominously overhead.

I slid from the bed and moved into the shower, washing up quickly before heading into the kitchen to make some coffee. While it brewed, I checked my messages.

I scowled as a woman's unfamiliar voice came over the line. Near the end, she added, almost as an afterthought, "It's Marina…It was nice talking to you earlier. Give me a call if you want to…talk a little more."

I hadn't needed the long, drawn-out paused to understand where she was getting. She had no desire to talk.

I had no desire to get tangled up with her. I deleted the message, wondering how she'd gotten my number.

There were four other messages, and I listened to them all before deleting them off the machine. That done, I poured myself a cup of coffee and went out on the back porch.

I lived in Lyons, Colorado in the house my parents had designed, and my father, with some help, had built the year before my birth. The house was a testament to his skill: craftsmanship showing in every line of the home, from the sparkling windows that went nearly from the ceiling to the floor in the living room to the lavish bath he'd built for my mother for their twentieth anniversary.

Their bedroom had sat empty for years.

The wreck that had killed them had altered the course of my life, and while I took care to keep everything clean and dust-free, I had no desire to live in that room.

My bedroom was the same one I'd used as a kid, and it had a wide window that faced out over the national park. There was also a door that opened onto the second-story balcony where I'd spent many a night doing homework at the wooden picnic bench that bisected the small space.

That balcony provided shelter from the rain from where I stood on the back porch, eyes on the skies as they were split apart by lightning.

The storm tugged at ugly memories, and I shoved them down, burying them before they had a chance to fully manifest. I'd spent most of the past night tossing and turning, sleeping only in snatches that were haunted by nightmares.

I wasn't going to court those nightmares a second night in a row. At least, not if I could help it.

Because I had so much trouble sleeping these days, I'd switched over to drinking decaf in the evenings and afternoons. I hadn't noticed much of a difference in my ability to sleep, even with cutting the caffeine out. Logically, I knew the reasons behind my lack of sleep, but it was just one more thing I didn't let myself acknowledge.

There was no point.

Either I'd sleep, or I wouldn't.

I'd gone days on just a couple of hours of sleep back when I was still in the service. It wouldn't kill me to go a day or two with only a couple hours of sleep a night.

The ringing of my phone drew my attention back to the house, and I headed inside, hoping it wasn't Marina. It was one of those nights, and I just might be tempted to give in.

But the number on the screen was a familiar one.

Picking up the phone, I answered, "Hello."

"Hey, it's me, honey."

"Hi, Cass." I put the coffee down and pinched the bridge of my nose. "How is your trip going?"

"Oh, it's fine. I wanted to let you know I'd be in sometime tomorrow, later in the evening, I'm afraid. But if it's not *too* late, maybe we can grab dinner tomorrow night."

"Yeah. Sure. That sounds good."

From the other end of the line, I heard a huge yawn, followed by a dry laugh. "Needless to say, I haven't slept much while I was gone."

"Sounds normal for you, Cass."

She made a noise of agreement, then said, "I'm going to turn in soon. I'll see you tomorrow, okay? I love you."

"Yeah, you too."

I disconnected the call and put the phone back in the cradle as the tension I'd been trying to fight off rose inside me once more.

THREE
LEXI

MORNING DAWNED BRIGHT AND CLEAR, THE BLUE BOWL OF the sky framing the tall spires of evergreens that thrust proudly upward. I was due to work the park until nine, so I didn't have to go in until eleven, and I was enjoying my coffee out on the back deck, staring up at the mountains. The temperature had dropped since last night, and I'd already checked the weather. This might be the last nice morning for the next few days.

As the forecast had anticipated, clouds were moving in, and they were calling for snow to start sometime this evening.

My phone buzzed, letting me know I had a message.

I grinned when I saw who it was from, my cousin and one of my best friends, Breanna Parrino. It had been a few weeks since we'd been able to get together, and we'd been texting back and forth, trying to plan out a camping trip once the weather was a little nicer.

Okay, can you manage to get off for a few days in May?

I considered it, then tapped in a response.

That's when things start getting busy. Might be better to plan it around one of my off-weekends and I can just request Friday off. You can't handle being away from society for more than a couple days anyway.

I laughed when her response came up.

I resemble that remark. So...I was thinking. Would you mind if Ryder came with me? I'd like you to get to know him better.

I'd met her new boyfriend only a few months earlier, and I had liked him well enough. I wasn't sure I wanted him crashing my time with my cousin, but I couldn't exactly say no, either. At least, not without feeling bad.

Sure, that's fine. As long as Mr. Mega-bucks realizes we're actually hiking. This isn't one of those rich people camping get-a-ways that have heated yurts and all that shit.

Breanna sent me back a laughing emoji.

He can probably outpace you, darling.

I rolled my eyes. As if. I checked the time on my phone and tapped back a quick response before finishing off my coffee.

I need to go. Gotta shower and get to work.

Breanna replied before I'd even escaped the message app.

Go stop those pic-a-nic basket stealing bears, cuz.

With a grin, I shoved the phone into my pocket and headed inside to shower.

THE MORNING PASSED SO FAST, I barely had time to blink. I had only just gotten inside and clocked in when a commotion exploded up front. I shoved my bag into my locker and headed out to find the source of the chaos.

A young woman with heavy plaits of dark hair was holding a little boy, and both were splashed with blood.

The blood was coming from his forehead, it looked like. She was holding something wadded up and shoved against the boy's brow, and from what I could tell, it was already soaking through.

I caught the eye of one of the rangers near her and jerked a thumb toward the back, letting him know I'd get the first aid kit.

I darted back through the employee only door and rushed down the hall. It only took a moment to find the over-sized kit. It looked more like a fishing tackle box than anything else, but the bright red box was stocked well-enough to take care of any number of minor accidents and emergencies. I also grabbed the box of gloves that was kept ready next to the kit.

Once back in the main area, I put the kit down and tugged a pair of gloves on, moving closer to the mom and son.

I caught the boy's dark eyes and gave him a sympathetic smile. He continued to wail. No doubt hurt, but I suspected he was also scared.

"It's going to be okay," I told him as I moved closer.

I was less than two feet away when a male form cut in front of me. "Hey there, little fella!"

I mentally grimaced at the familiar voice and braced myself as a fellow ranger and all-around asshole, Stilwell Jenner, started speaking to the boy, his voice big and booming.

"Jenner," a firm voice said from the other side of the counter.

I flicked a look at our supervisor who was staring pointedly at Jenner's ungloved hands.

As he glanced down, trying to see what the problem was, I grabbed the kit and moved around him.

The panicking mom saw me and her eyes, bright with unshed tears, focused on the red kit I was carrying.

"Are you a paramedic or something?" she demanded.

"I'm a little bit of everything," I told her. "I've had the basic EMT training, and I took a few other courses. If you'll let me, I'll look at your little guy there."

She nodded, almost desperately.

"Come on," I said, gesturing her over to the nearest chair.

It happened to be behind the main desk, and as she sat down, one of the other rangers brought me a seat as well. I kicked it closer and put the kit down on the counter, giving the little boy a gentle smile.

His panicked cries had calmed somewhat, and now that his mother was getting herself together, he seemed to settle even more. I flipped open the kit and riffled through it, pulling out what I thought I'd need as I spoke to the mother.

"Did he trip and smack his head on something?"

"Yes." She took a deep, shaky breath before continuing, "He hit the corner of a bench out front. He was running – he saw a lady with a companion dog, and he wanted to pet him. I went chasing after him, but I wasn't fast enough."

"It's amazing how fast these little guys can be, isn't it?" I gave her a reassuring smile as I tore open a couple of large gauze pads. "Okay, let's take a look."

Sensing somebody behind me, I darted a look over my shoulder, hoping it wasn't Stilwell. To my relief, I met the faded gray eyes of my supervisor, Lance Hawthorne. I redirected my attention back to the boy and his mother. I gestured for her to remove the cloth she'd shoved against it — a shirt, from what I could tell.

As soon as she pulled it away, the blood started seeping from the small, jagged laceration on the child's forehead. "Why won't it stop bleeding?" she said, her voice terribly small and scared.

"Head wounds always bleed a lot," I assured her. I pressed the gauze to the injury, soaking up the fresh blood and tentatively clearing the area around it so I could take a look. "Honey, you're going to have quite a goose egg there."

He struggled in his mother's arms, and she tightened her grip. "Be still, Devonté," she chided. "Be still and let the nice lady take care of you."

He continued to squirm and cry softly, and she gave me an apologetic look.

"It's fine." I swiped another piece of gauze across his skin, clearing away a little more blood.

"I've got something I can use to close the wound for now, but I think you should get him looked at by the local ER. He could probably use a couple of stitches."

Panic tightened her features again, and I gave her a reassuring smile. "It will be okay. I doubt he'll need more than a few."

By the time the local paramedics arrived to ferry Mama and child to the closest ER a good thirty minutes away, the boy had stopped crying and had fallen asleep. His mother looked like she could use a nap too. She looked completely overwhelmed.

It was an expression I'd seen before, and usually in similar circumstances. A nice day at the park ruined after tripping and twisting an ankle, a camping accident that resulted in a burned hand. This was the third time in the eighteen months I'd been with the park that a child had come in with his head busted open after tripping and falling, hitting something.

As I was gathering up the trash, Stilwell came up to stand next to me. "You know, he probably didn't need to go to the emergency room, Alex," he said, his voice condescending as usual. "You overreacted, and you're going to cost that family quite a bit of money over a little scratch."

I slanted a look at him, irritation bubbling up inside. The reasons for my ire was two-fold. Stilwell had only basic CPR and first aid training, so he really wasn't in any position to be questioning me in this area. And...my name wasn't *Alex*.

I gave him a short look. "The name is *Lexi*, Stilwell. Why is it so hard for you to remember that?"

"Sorry." He said it without sincerity and continued on to say, "It just seems...well, you wanted to work in this field. Seems the name *Alex* would suit you better."

I didn't bother responding to that comment. He'd made it more than clear that he didn't think women belonged in 'manly' fields, like being law enforcement officers, doctors, lawyers...or rangers. Women belonged in front of a classroom, taking orders from a *male* doctor, or at home in the kitchen cooking.

I wasn't just *speculating* on that, either. He'd made it more than clear that he believed those very things.

I believed Stilwell was an asshole and not one I wanted to be bothered with. Sadly, I too often got hooked up with him as we patrolled the park, and today would be another one of those days.

"You did a good job, Lexi."

At my supervisor's words, I looked up and nodded. "Thank you, sir."

"Hawthorne," Stilwell started in an ingratiating voice, "it's not very likely that kid needed to get stitches, or ride in an ambulance—"

"I thought you opted out of the advanced first aid training we provide," Hawthorne said, directing his attention toward Stilwell.

Stilwell cleared his throat. "It doesn't take a medical degree to know that head wounds can be scary, but *scary* doesn't mean *emergency*."

"Uh-huh." Hawthorne studied Stilwell for a minute. "Well, in this case, I think erring on the side of safety is the better option. The kid's poor mom was shaking so bad, she could have very well driven off the road and not realized it until it was too late."

Stilwell looked like he wanted to say something else, but Hawthorne shifted his attention back to me. "As I said, good job, Lexi. Appreciate the level head and quick work." He checked his watch, then nodded at us. "It's about time for the two of you to hit the road."

ALTHOUGH I'D EXPECTED IT, Stilwell was more of an ass than usual, thanks to the morning's events. He was driving with far too much recklessness as we did patrol, taking corners far sharper than needed and speeding around the vehicles of the park guests who were out trying to enjoy the chilly spring day before another snow moved in.

By the time we were ready to eat our lunch, I was convinced I'd rather hike the entire rest of the way back than climb into the Jeep with Stilwell for even five more minutes.

Sadly, I didn't have that option. We still had to finish up our route and check a few camp areas before heading back. Hoofing it on my own just wasn't viable.

The temperature continued to drop throughout the day, and by the time we were at the last campsite on our route, it was downright cold. My breath came out in a puffy plume as I walked the perimeter of the now vacated camp. We'd had to give weather warnings to several die-hard outdoor lovers, but for the most part, few wanted to stay overnight when there was a snow forecasted.

"That was a fat waste of time," Stilwell announced from behind the steering wheel as I slid into the Jeep. I'd just finished making my rounds about the camp while he stayed in the nice, warm vehicle. "It's pretty obvious nobody is here."

I bared my teeth at him in a sharp-edged smile. "We visit the campsites for more than just informing visitors about the weather," I reminded him.

He rolled his eyes.

I ignored him and reached into one of the zippered pockets on my coat, fishing out my gloves. As I tugged them on, I listened to the updates and chatter coming from the radio. All the park vehicles were equipped with one. There were a lot of areas in the park that didn't have cell phone towers, and the most reliable way to communicate was via radio.

There were reports of a lost child, and Stilwell groaned as I turned up the volume to listen. As I tried to focus on the report being given, Stilwell complained. That was nothing new – he *always* complained, but today's complaints seemed mostly centered around kids and why so much work was dumped on us because of irresponsible parents.

"You've never seen how fast a four-year-old can move," I said in a dry tone after listening to him vent for nearly five minutes.

"No four-year-old can move faster than *I* can," he stated. "If these people would just watch their kids better…"

The radio crackled, and he lapsed into silence as I turned the volume up a little more. The words were half-lost in the static.

But soon a grin spread across my face.

"Child has been located."

Stilwell snorted. "Sure was lost. The alert went out all of ten minutes ago. Walk around for five minutes, then give up and call us?"

I personally would rather parents do that than risk wasting precious minutes that could be used to locate the child – or risk the parents getting lost on top of the kid.

But I kept my opinion to myself.

Settling more comfortably into the faux-leather of the seat, I crossed my arms over my chest and stared out at the terrain that was slowly becoming more and more familiar to me. After eighteen months of living right at the base of the Rockies, I was still in awe of the beauty of this place. I'd grown up in Colorado Springs and had been surrounded by these mountains all my life. And still, every day, I fell a little more in love.

Stilwell griped for another couple of minutes, but when I didn't respond, he also lapsed into silence, letting me enjoy the rest of the drive back.

It took almost forty-five minutes, and by the time we parked the Jeep, clouds had gathered overhead, an ominous display that left me wondering just how much snow might get dumped on us. Although there were still a couple of hours before sunset, the clouds made it far darker than normal for this time of year.

The wind whipped at my ponytail as I headed inside, not bothering to wait for Stilwell. I had to take care of my paperwork for the day before relieving Amy at the desk in the visitor's center.

It was promising to be a boring evening, as evidenced by several of my fellow rangers milling around the center, talking to each other or checking their phones. I saw only two visitors. They looked to be a couple, and Amy was talking to them, her bright, animated face more reserved than normal.

The couple turned to leave, and I caught sight of the crestfallen look on the woman's face.

"Weren't prepared for snow, huh?" I asked Amy as I moved behind the counter. It felt good to be out of the Jeep and not just because it got me away from Stilwell.

"Nope," she said cheerily. She continued to stare out the window, and I followed her gaze. We both breathed a sigh of relief as the couple backed out, then headed back in the direction of the park entrance and Estes Park.

"Thank God," Amy muttered. "I don't think anybody wants to be looking for a couple of lost tourists tonight or tomorrow."

I nodded my agreement as Amy maneuvered her wheelchair out from behind the main desk.

"Hold up, Amy," Hawthorne said as he pushed through the door separating the visitor's area from the employee space. "Can you hang around a while longer?"

She made a face. "I can. The question is…*will I?*"

"Will you?" he asked. No smile cracked his face as he nodded at me. "I need Lexi and all other hands on deck. We just got a report of a small private plane going down not too far from here."

"Again?" Stilwell said, disgust in his voice.

Amy sighed and pushed her hair back from her face. "I can handle the front desk."

As I passed by her, I rested a hand on her shoulder. She looked up at me with a faint smile. "Guess we spoke too soon, didn't we?"

"Yup." I headed toward the back, not bothering to wait for Hawthorne who'd moved to speak with Stilwell. I swear, if I got paired with him for a search and rescue, I was going to rip my hair out.

FOUR

ROMAN

I SHOULD HAVE DONE THIS SHIT EARLIER.

The temperature had been dropping throughout the day, and by the way the sky looked, I could tell we were in for at least one more snow before winter was done with us. Although I doubted it would be anything serious, I wasn't going to chance running out of wood, either.

I had a generator in case the electricity went out, but I knew from experience it wasn't a good idea to have just one back-up. Generators ran on gas, after all, and I didn't exactly live in town. If I ran out of gas, I could be seriously fucked without another source of heat.

Besides, I had only so many things I could do to keep my mind occupied.

Bringing the ax down on the log, I tried to blank my mind. It wasn't easy. If my parents hadn't been killed in that car wreck eighteen years ago, their fortieth wedding anniversary would have been today. But they were gone, just like everybody else in my life.

Not everybody, I reminded myself. Cass was still there. Thinking of her had me checking the time. I still had close to two hours before I had to leave for the airport. Shooting another look at the sky, I hoped the weather held long enough for them to land. Cass was coming in on a small private plane I'd helped her charter for a job in Jackson, Wyoming.

She was trying to build up a customer base as an event coordinator, and a friend of her family had hired her to handle a wedding. There was a catch, of course. The wedding was in Jackson, and the bride had asked her if she could travel there for a few of the meetings. The bride's family was as rich as Croesus, and both the bride and her mother had assured Cass that she'd be reimbursed, but she hadn't wanted to let them know she didn't have the capital or the credit to cover the initial expense.

I'd already offered to give her some operating capital, but she hadn't accepted. She did relent some when I pressed for her to let me handle chartering the plane, although she insisted she'd pay me back.

I'd have been happier to get her on a commercial flight, but the bride hadn't wanted to wait so we'd gone the private route.

I didn't like *big* planes, much less, small ones. I knew all the safety stats for aircraft, large and small, but even though I'd traveled that way all over the world multiple times, I still didn't care for planes. I like my feet on the ground. I also liked for the people I cared about to keep their feet on the ground.

Telling myself not to worry about it, I finished splitting

the log and tossed the halves onto the pile at my right. I grabbed another and started the process all over again.

Despite my attempts to block out any sort of thought beyond the focus needed for the task before me, my mind kept wandering back. I could remember times my parents had celebrated their marriage, Mom dressed up in her best dress while Dad wore the suit she'd nagged him into donning, them smiling on their way out the door.

They'd been smiling like that the last time we saw them.

That thought had me fumbling, and I stopped mid-swing. With a growl, I drove the blade of the ax into the tree stump under the log. I turned away from the log and shoved overlong hair out of my eyes.

Brooding, I stared out over the land in front of me. This piece of property had been in my family for generations. Next to Cass, this was the only thing in the world that mattered to me. But sometimes, I hated being there.

There were too many memories in this place.

Everywhere I looked, I saw something that elicited a new memory, something that made me…ache.

Times when we'd gone camping in those mountains that punched up into the sky around me. Fall nights when we'd all sat out in the backyard, a fire crackling in the firepit where we all roasted marshmallows. Riding the horses across the empty miles that stretched out all around us.

Riding in a bus…

"Stop it," I muttered.

But the memories wouldn't stop playing through my mind, an endless strip of them, one right after the other.

Knowing I was too distracted to keep using the ax, I grabbed some logs and trekked across the wide stretch of grass between me and the house. There was a woodpile on the back porch, protected from rain and snow by the second story deck that ran the width of the house. It was running low now, but the wood I'd chopped today would be enough to last a couple of weeks, even if the power did go out.

By the time I had hauled all the wood to the porch and put away my tools, it was late enough that I needed to start getting ready for the drive into Boulder. Although Cass wasn't scheduled to land for a while longer, I'd have to go through the Boulder area right around rush hour, and I'd rather get into town earlier and find some place to get a beer while I waited.

I was already looking forward to several beers.

If I didn't have to take care of picking up Cass, I'd probably already be digging up a bottle of Tennessee whiskey. I'd spent way too many nights like that up until I took a job working as a night-time security guard at one of the big banks in Denver a few nights a week.

It had been the drinking that had pushed me to get a job in the first place. I'd spent more than a decade in the army and had rarely spent any of the paychecks I'd earned, banking them for a future that no longer mattered. It left me with enough money that I could have gone several more years without needing a job, since the home and land where I lived was paid off. Even my truck was paid off, a vehicle I'd bought on a whim on one of my trips back home.

With a job, I had less time to do the needed work around the property, which in turn kept me busier on the days I wasn't working.

That was just the way I liked it.

The busier I was, the less time I had to think.

To remember.

BEFORE GOING TO SHOWER, I went to check on the horses. We used to have four of them, but the two that had belonged to my parents died several years back.

Hellboy and Captain, named for our favorite comic heroes, were now twenty-six years old, bought for us as Christmas presents when we were kids. Although I didn't take as much pleasure in riding as I used to, I still babied them as much as I had when we'd gotten them.

I'd just brushed them out yesterday and fed them this morning, but since I had to take care of picking up Cass from the municipal airport in Boulder, I figured I'd be late getting in.

I made sure they had plenty of food and water, then spent a few minutes just talking to them and scratching under the coarse hair of their manes. Captain nudged me in the belly with her nose which had Hellboy whickering at me in an attempt, to get my attention.

I went over to him and gave him some affection.

Even though there were a lot of memories in the barn and with the horses that could tangle me up, this was the one place on the property where I found some level of peace. I probably didn't deserve it, and more than once, I'd considered selling the horses.

But in the end, I never could do it.

As I talked to the animals, time slipped away, and I ended up spending far more time in the barn than I should have.

I hurried through locking up the barn and headed inside, going straight up the steps to the small shower that joined the two upstairs bedrooms.

There was a larger bathroom off the master bedroom, but I hadn't used it, even once, since I'd moved back in.

I made quick work of washing up and pondered the idea of shaving, but in the end, didn't feel like messing with it. It wasn't like Cass would care, and I definitely didn't.

My hair was still damp when I climbed into my truck fifteen minutes later. My stomach grumbled, reminding me that I hadn't eaten anything since I'd crawled out of bed at noon.

I checked the time and decided I'd still get to the airport before Cass landed, so I stopped at a fast-food joint after entering Lyons and got a burger and soft drink.

By the time I was heading down Highway 36 toward Boulder, I figured I'd get to the airport just before Cass landed.

So much for getting a drink or two. But I'd make up for it tonight after I took care of Cass.

The mountain peaks around me were all but lost in the clouds that had been piling up all day. I eyed them with more than a little trepidation. Not for me, but the pilot flying Cass and her assistant home had to fly and land in that mess. The wind was whipping hard enough that I could hear it even though the windows were up, causing the younger trees around me to sway from the intensity.

The weather was getting worse too. Shooting a look at the clock, I tried not to let myself get anxious as I sped down the highway. Turning on the radio, I let the strains of some random country ballad fill the air.

I'd finally managed to calm myself when my cell phone chimed. I grabbed it and saw that it was from Cass. Glancing at the road, I swiped my thumb over the screen. Had she gotten in already?

I skimmed the message.

Shock punched at me.

The truck started to veer, and I jerked my gaze up as somebody blasted their horn at me.

Swearing, I pulled over on the side of the road and stared at the message, not entirely comprehending.

Something's gone wrong. I love you, Roman.

"What the fuck?" I whispered. I punched in a demand that she answer but there was no response.

Dread choked me, fear whispering in the back of my head.

I sent a second message, and five minutes later, a third.

She never answered.

I DIDN'T KNOW how long I sat there on the side of the road, staring at the blank screen of my phone and waiting for some response from Cass.

Easily twenty minutes had passed, though. If things had worked as they should have, Cass would be landing in just a few minutes. Just the thought of that made me look at the phone.

Something's gone wrong, she'd told me.

I grabbed the phone and hit the browser to pull up the information for the charter service we'd selected.

A song on the radio stopped as I found the number.

Just as I hit the first number, a voice came over the station in lieu of the music. "We're getting reports of a small plane going down in the park in the region of Estes Park."

Everything else the DJ said fell on deaf ears as I looked back at the phone I held in my hand.

Something's gone wrong. I love you, Roman.

Panicked, I hit the phone icon to try and call her.

The phone rang and rang, then finally went to voicemail.

FIVE
LEXI

"I HEAR YOU'RE GOING OUT WITH US."

At that voice, I looked up from the pack I'd been checking. As one of the members of a local search and rescue group, I'd been on four SARs already, but this was the first time I'd had to help search for passengers of a downed plane. We weren't sure what we'd find since we hadn't heard from anybody onboard the craft.

From what I could tell, that had the more experienced searchers concerned. I understood why. A plane, even small-engine crafts, were equipped with radios that would allow them to alert officials to their status and give updates on injuries, not to mention hopefully being able to offer a more detailed description of their location.

With the snow that had moved in, we couldn't bring in support from local pilots who were experienced in visual searches of the terrain from above. If we didn't find them tonight, we hoped the weather would clear by the morning, so the pilots could help out.

One of those pilots was the man in front of me, Roger Chadwick. He was the one who'd led the SAR course I'd taken not long after being hired for my current position with the national park. I'd also known him from talks he'd given at Colorado State University. He used to work with the National Parks System but had quit to focus more on search and rescue. We'd talked several times when he was at CSU, and it was his recommendation, I suspected, that had gotten me hired at the park. It was harder than hell to get a job at most national parks and even harder to get one at the park here in the Rockies.

"Roger!" I greeted him with a quick hug.

He returned the hug and stepped back, gesturing for me to continue with my check of the bag.

"You said *us*," I said as I continued the important process. Multi-tool, fireproof container for my lighter and matches – I never went without both – headlamp, a big piece of coated nylon I could use to make shelter, food, several different over-the-counter meds. "Does that mean one of your partners will handle any visual searches tomorrow?"

"Yep." He ran a hand over his hair. "I think I'm better suited to help with the ground search in this case since I spent more than a decade working in this area."

"I'll be glad to have you. If you're going out with us, who's the incident commander?"

He gestured to a tall, thin woman standing with Hawthorne in front of a large-scale map of the local area. "Hailey Sims is IC this time around. Ever met her?"

I shook my head, still focused on the pack in front of me. When it was completely packed, as it was now, the backpack weighed roughly thirty pounds. It would sustain me for more than a day easily, although I was hoping I wouldn't be out that long.

"Roger!"

I grimaced as a shadow fell over my pack, letting me know that Stilwell had quietly come up behind me and was now standing a lot closer than I liked.

"Stilwell," Roger said in a neutral voice.

I'd seen the two men working together on two of the SARs I'd been on, and I had the feeling that Roger didn't much like the other man. I couldn't say I blamed him. Stilwell was so easy to *dis*like. It was like he made a study of it.

"Alex are you sure you can handle a search like this?" Stilwell asked, shifting his attention to me.

I bit my tongue against the urge to remind him that it wasn't *Alex*. My dad had been Alex. Hearing his name, even almost two years after his death, was enough to make my heart pang. But if I let on that it bothered me, Stilwell would just keep it up so instead of snapping at him like I wanted, I told him flatly, "I think I can handle it. It's not like I haven't gone out before."

"Still…" He blew out a breath, and I could all but *feel* the condescension raining down on me. "Nighttime searches are rough, and they're even harder in weather like this."

"I appreciate the concern," I said with false sweetness.

Across from me, Roger made a choking sound which quickly turned into a cough. I shot him a look in time to see him covering his mouth with his fist. But his eyes were laughing. Since Stilwell couldn't easily see my face from his position, I rolled my eyes at Roger, who then started to cough even harder.

Stilwell, ever helpful, asked, "Are you okay, Roger? Want Alex to get you some water?"

Why don't you get him some water, you asshat? I kept the snide comment behind my teeth, though.

"She's finishing her gear check," Roger said, voice slightly strained. "Speaking of which, if you haven't finished your double-check, you need to get to it. The first teams are heading out soon."

"Oh, I think I'm good. Alex, did you pack enough clothing and water?"

I clenched my jaw and gave him a short nod, still not looking at him. I swear, if he kept calling me *Alex*...

I cut the thought off. He'd keep doing it, and I'd just keep ignoring him and acting like it didn't matter. I could always say something to Hawthorne, but that would just make matters worse, I suspected. Besides, it seemed...petty. It wasn't, not to me, but I could easily imagine how others would view it as such.

Apparently, he realized I wasn't going to rise to the bait because Stilwell shifted his focus to Roger. "Glad to have you on hand as IC for this one, Roger. Your experience will come in handy."

"Oh, I'm not in charge this time around. I'll be out there with the rest of the teams."

Because I already knew how he'd act, I looked up as Stilwell. "Who is handling it? I haven't seen Brad anywhere."

Brad was another one of Roger's partners and often took over as IC when Roger was either unavailable or up in his little Cessna, offering support through visual searches.

"No. Brad's not on tonight. My other partner, Hailey Sims, is working as IC this time around."

Stilwell blinked. The lines near his eyes tightened a fraction and a muscle pulsed once in his jaw. "Hailey," he said slowly. "I don't think I've ever worked with her."

"She's a newer addition to the group." Roger's eyes danced with humor that likely went unnoticed by Stilwell. "She's a total ass-kicker, too, just so you know. Search and rescue is her life."

Roger jabbed a thumb over his shoulder, directing Stilwell to where Hailey still stood with Hawthorne. "She's over there talking to your boss if you want to go introduce yourself."

As if. I hid a smile and looked back down at my pack, then checked the list I kept on hand. Everything was in there.

"Thanks, but I shouldn't interrupt them."

As he walked off, I glanced up at Roger.

He met my eyes and asked, "How do you work with that clown?"

"That's something I wonder daily."

Roger grinned, his blue-green eyes crinkling around the corners. "As much as I hate it, Stilwell is going to be on my team."

I made a face. "But I wanted to be on your team."

"I'd much rather have you than him, and you're welcome to join up with us, but I need Stilwell where I can keep an eye on him. There have been a few times where he's been more of a hindrance than a help." He shoved a hand through dark hair that was starting to silver at the temples. "At least if he's with me, he'll shut up when I tell him to. He won't give some of the other team leaders the same respect."

"That's just *shocking* to hear," I said, deadpan. "I can't imagine Stilwell ever doing anything that wasn't *respectful*."

"I think you meant *disrespectful*...Alex."

I made a face at him, and he laughed. "I assume you've already told him that you prefer to go by Lexi and he's just being an asshole?"

"You assume correctly." I sighed and grabbed a ponytail holder from the side pocket of my pack, scooping my hair up in a tight, low tail so the strawberry blonde strands wouldn't blow in my face once we got out in the cold.

I could hear the wind even from inside the ranger station near the Wild Basin park entrance. The SAR would be based out of here, the easiest station to access near the area where we believed the plane had gone down. We had a seriously large area we had to cover, and it was going to be done in the wet, clumpy snow that had started falling nearly an hour ago.

The past few weeks had been starting to warm up which would prove to be both a blessing and curse during the upcoming search. Since it had been warm, it would take a much heavier snowfall for it to accumulate enough to impede the search. But because it had been warm, the ground was no longer frozen, and the snow and mud could make for treacherous footing.

Up near the front of the station, Hailey put her fingers to her lips and let out a sharp whistle.

Silence fell through the station as, one by one, each of the rangers and SAR volunteers turned to face Hailey.

"Okay, guys. It's probably going to be a long, wet, messy night," she announced. "Gather round if you don't mind.

I'm going to give you what info we have, then we'll be heading out."

She spoke with a slow, lazy drawl that softened her *Rs* and *Gs*. It was a comforting, confident sort of voice, and her eyes were watchful and sharp. As everybody moved closer at the IC's request, I glanced outside at the snow. Fat flakes were already affecting visibility. I had no doubt that she'd hit the nail on the head when she predicted a long, wet, messy night.

"I've spoken to Hawthorne." She gestured to the man standing next to her, his arms folded across a wide chest. "The two of us are going to man the station and keep everybody updated. We've already got you broken down into teams. You guys will be the first SAR teams going out, and it's my hope that one of you will find the plane before we need to bring in more people." She paused a moment, letting everybody process her words. "But considering the weather and the fact that we've yet to contact anybody involved in the crash, we're working against the clock. Other teams are already being mobilized and will be ready to head out the minute we put out the call."

"Do we even know if there are any survivors?" Stilwell asked.

Hailey looked over at him. "As I've pointed out, we've yet to contact anybody from the plane so it's hard to say if there are survivors or not. Regardless, we've got a job to do."

"Do we know—"

Hailey cut in, her voice firm without coming off as rude. "I'm sure you'll understand…" She glanced at Hawthorne.

"Stilwell Jenner," Hawthorne supplied.

"Thank you. Stilwell, I'm sure you understand how essential it is to get out there, so please hold all your questions until I'm done. That goes for the group. If I fail to address your concerns as I go through the information we have available, I'll be sure to do that once we wrap up and break into our individual teams."

From where I stood, I had a good view of Stilwell, and as Hailey went back to addressing the group, I caught sight of his expression.

He could have been force-fed a hive of bees and looked happier than he did in that moment.

SIX

ROMAN

The drive from Lyons to the Wild Basin entrance took about an hour.

It was one of the longest damn hours of my life, and when I finally reached the station where I'd heard the SAR teams would be assembling, I was about ready to come out of my skin.

I wasn't exactly dressed for helping with any kind of search, but I did keep a pack of essentials in my truck, a habit my father had drilled into us after he had engine trouble one night and ended up practically freezing to death in his car back in his twenties.

All the missions I'd gone on as a Ranger in the army had furthered my knowledge on what I'd need to survive in any given situation, and I never left the house without that pack in my truck.

I parked in the spot farthest from the station with the driver's side of the truck facing away from the group. After grabbing the pack and digging out what I currently needed,

I swiftly unlaced my boots, then kicked them off and shucked my jeans. I had a set of cold-weather gear that would work as a base layer under my jeans and the two shirts I already wore, a thermal with a flannel thrown over the top. The battered leather coat I'd worn out of the house was waterproofed, but it wasn't ideal for this kind of weather. I'd survive, though. I'd been in worse with far less protection than I had available to me in the pack.

After sliding into the thin but warm pants, I pulled my jeans and boots back on and then stripped out of my coat and the shirts to don the heat-retaining shirt. I'd used this gear when I was in the army and knew just how well it insulated. Although the jeans I wore weren't exactly ideal, they'd be good enough if the temperature didn't drop another twenty degrees or so. I realized that was still a possibility and double-checked to make sure I had adequate clothes tucked away inside my pack. I should probably take a few minutes to change into those, but I could see through the passenger window that the rangers and various volunteers were already breaking up into groups.

After hauling my bag out and settling it into place, I started for the clusters of people gathered outside the small log building that now served as a station for the forest rangers.

There was a tall, athletic-looking guy standing on the outskirts without a pack, and I homed in on him. He wore the easily recognizable uniform of a park ranger and stood with his hands on his hips, staring at the commotion going on around him.

Since he wasn't already wearing a pack and his coat hung open, it was likely he wasn't joining the search. That meant he'd be one of the support personnel and should be able to point me to whoever was in charge. Maybe I'd luck out, and he'd be the one I needed to talk to — and preferably, he'd be open to what I had to say.

It didn't matter in the long run, because I was going out to look for Cass. Nothing was changing that.

"Hey," I said, nodding at him as I approached.

He skimmed me up and down. "If you're here as one of the volunteers, you're pushing it. It's about time to head out."

"Yeah, I'm here to help with the search," I said, not outright denying that I was a volunteer. He'd offered the opening, so I might as well take it. "Are you in charge here?"

"No," he replied in a short, tight voice. "Sadly, I'm not." He studied me more closely, eyes sliding to the scar on my cheek before connecting with mine once more. "I don't recall seeing you with any of the SAR volunteer groups before."

"No, you haven't," I responded. "Who is in charge, then?"

He didn't answer that question. Instead, he fired one of his own at me. "Are you with one of the local SAR groups?" His eyes trailed to the scar again, and he made no attempt to hide his study of it.

"No, I'm not."

His pale blue eyes shot to mine, brows dropping low. His face folded into a tight scowl. "Are you trying to be difficult?"

"Not especially." I wondered if he was trying to be an ass. If so, he was succeeding. I didn't point that out to him though. Instead, I admitted, "I'm the one who chartered the plane that crashed. I've got somebody out there, and I'm going to help find her."

"That's not advised," he said with a disdainful look. "This is dangerous work for experienced searchers only."

I wasn't about to tell him that he didn't know shit about danger but figured that wouldn't make things any easier. "Look, I'm joining the search with or without a team, so you might as well help me out."

"Fine." He heaved out a sigh. "It's your funeral."

"So…who can I talk to?"

He gave me a sour look, then skimmed the throng around us. "I don't…there." He pointed across the lot. "See the blonde? That's Alex. Go talk to her. She'll help you out. If you're that determined to go out, maybe she can take you to the crash site."

I turned to look for who he might be talking to. The only blonde I saw was a curvy little powerhouse in the process of pulling on a heavy coat. The coat quickly hid those curves, but I'd already taken in the long legs and how well she filled out the front of her uniform shirt. Her hair was gathered into a ponytail which she freed from the collar of the coat before pulling something from the coat's pocket. I watched as she drew on a knit cap.

A man, clad in clothing that made it clear he wasn't one of the park rangers, approached her and they talked for a few minutes, giving me the chance to study her.

She was beautiful. I felt a flicker of interest, which I immediately smashed down until it blinked out of existence. She was also young. I figured she was easily ten years younger than me, although she held herself with a certain confidence as she looked around the commotion taking place before looking back at her companion and giving a decisive nod.

I guess she'd have to have a fair amount of confidence to do what she did. Search-and-rescue missions weren't for the faint-hearted.

I glanced back, looking for the guy I'd been talking to and found him already involved in another conversation. From what I could hear, he sounded like he was lecturing the woman standing in front of him, telling her she probably wasn't prepared for the mess they had ahead of them. And he wasn't doing it nicely, either. I didn't much care about being nice myself, but this guy came off as a complete prick.

SEVEN

LEXI

Roger left me to return to his group, and I looked around, taking stock of the group I was working with.

I was damn glad that Stilwell was in the one Roger would be leading out and not mine, although it would have been nice to work with one of my former mentors.

I brushed the thought aside, reminding myself that this wasn't a social gig, even if I was in the midst of the sort of people I felt most comfortable with.

Crouching down in front of my bag, I rifled through the outer pockets, checking a few last-minute items, then making sure all the compartments were zipped.

A pair of large booted feet appeared in my line of vision, and I looked up just as a deep voice asked, "Excuse me. Are you Alex?"

I tilted my head back and looked up, and up, and up. I found myself staring into a pair of pale green eyes, sharp as jagged ice and burning with intensity. Slowly, I rose. I was five-foot-six, not at all short, and the thick-soled hiking boots

I wore gave me another inch, but even with that added height, I had to tip my head back to meet the gaze of the man standing in front of me.

"It's not Alex," I said levelly, although there was a strange flutter in my chest, one I didn't recognize immediately. It was attraction, deep, immediate, intense attraction, the kind I rarely felt, and I hadn't experienced it at all for several years. Still, I managed to quash it down and continue, "I go by Lexi. Can I help you?"

Before the man had a chance to respond, Stilwell was at my side, his smarmy smile firmly fixed in place. "Alex," he said, gesturing to the man in front of me. "This guy says he's the one who rented the plane that went down. He wants to join in with the search group. I told him you'd be the best bet to take him out to the crash site."

My jaw fell open. I immediately snapped it closed and focused a hot glare on Stilwell. I was not the best bet to do any such thing. That stupid prick. He always had to do something to cause me trouble.

He reached out to pat my shoulder, and because there was somebody else standing there, I didn't smack his hand away. One of these days, though, he'd put a hand on me, and I'd break it off at the wrist and maybe feed it to him for good measure.

"I better go join my crew," Stilwell said with a cheerful smile. "You two be safe."

He turned on his heel, leaving me behind stewing with fury. It was a little surprising smoke wasn't coming out of my ears as I turned my attention to the newcomer.

"What's your name, sir?" I asked, managing to keep my voice level through sheer force of will.

"It's Roman Sayers."

I stuck my hand out, and he immediately accepted, giving me a firm handshake. Something jolted in my belly, and I quickly tugged my hand free, resisting the urge to rub my palm with my fingers. "Mr. Sayers—"

"Roman," he corrected.

I nodded. "Roman, then. I'm not sure what Stilwell was getting at, but there's no way I can take you out to the crash site. We haven't even located it. We just have a general area. We'll be fanning out to start the search, and it's going to be a hard, cold night."

"I've been cold before," he replied, looking unperturbed.

"It's a lot more than just *being cold*," I said, crossing my arms over my chest and staring him down. "Let me be blunt, Mr...Roman," I corrected. "This will be a hard search, and we have no idea what we're going to find. It's cold, and the snow isn't going to stop any time soon. We've got a large area to cover, and I don't have time for you. You'll get in the way." I softened my voice. "It will be best if you just let us do our jobs."

He cocked his head as I spoke, and when I was finished, he pinned me with a hard look. "I'm a former Ranger, ma'am. This will be a walk in the park...literally."

"You're a ranger?" I asked, looking him up and down skeptically. "What park did you work?"

He shook his head. "You misunderstand. I'm not a *park* ranger. I'm a former *Army Ranger* – big R. As in I've parachuted into areas that make this place look like a vacation spot and I've done things a lot more intense than look for a downed plane." He looked me up and down, then added,

"If anything, *I* don't have time for *you*, but I'm trying to be courteous here."

"This is what you call *courtesy*?" I snapped without even thinking about it.

"Maybe I'm out of practice." He shrugged, clearly unconcerned.

"Maybe." I huffed out a breath as I studied him. "Look, this is more than just walking and hiking and knowing how to handle rough terrain. You have to know the park–"

"I've lived in Lyons all my life and have probably spent more time here than some of the employees. Trust me, I know the park."

Trust him. Because I was on the job and *courtesy* was sort of required, I didn't give him the sneer I wanted to. I was going to punch Stilwell for getting me into this. I struggled to come up with the right way to convince him to stay here and wait for us, but for him, I must have been too quiet for too long.

He jabbed a thumb over his shoulder in the direction I'd been told to cover and said, "I'm going out, with or without you. And I'm going now."

"Look," I said, floundering. "Let me run this by the IC – that's the incident commander. She's in charge, and if she's cool with you going out with us, we can make this work. But I need to talk to her."

I looked around for Hailey and saw that my team was gathering up. Swearing, I shot a glance back at Roman, then pointed at the ground. "Stay here. I need a few minutes."

I didn't bother waiting to see if he'd listen, just hitched my bag up onto my shoulders. I settled in place as I moved over to my team and the two I'd be scheduled to work with. "I'll catch up. I have to handle something first."

That got me a skeptical look from the older of the two men. One was an experienced SAR volunteer, and the other was a park ranger who'd been on the job for almost as long as I'd been alive. Rafe Menendez was a tough piece of work, and I knew I wouldn't make him happy to not move out with them. "We need to get a move on, Lexi," he said, shaking his head.

"I know. Like I said, head on out and I'll catch up. This won't take long." *I hope.* I kept that last bit behind my teeth and plastered a confident smile on my face.

Without giving him a chance to ask me what was going on, I turned away and headed in the direction I'd last seen Hailey.

I found her and brought her up to speed, but when I went to point Roman out, I saw that he wasn't there. In an effort to see better, I squinted my eyes and peered through the fat, fluffy snowflakes. I thought I caught a glimpse of him near a big truck at the far end of the parking lot, but I couldn't be sure. It was completely dark now, and the area wasn't exactly well-lit.

"Looks like he changed his mind," Hailey said in a dry voice. She gave me a no-nonsense look then brushed past me.

"I'll look around the area for him, Lexi, but you need to join your crew."

I huffed out a breath and skimmed the area, catching sight of the two men I was supposed to hook up with as they pulled out of the parking lot. Logic told me to just flag them down and join them. If that jerk had gone out solo, it wouldn't be because I hadn't warned him.

A flicker of red caught my attention, and I looked over to see the big truck from the edge of the parking lot reversing.

For reasons unknown to me, I found myself striding across the pavement and placing my body exactly where he'd be driving if he was really dead-set on joining the search. I'd ride along with him to our area and convince him that we needed to hook up with the others.

At least that was the plan.

"I TOLD YOU TO *WAIT*," I said sourly as I swung into the truck next to him.

He cocked a brow. "I wasn't aware I was taking orders from you, princess."

The *princess* comment stunned me into silence for maybe ten seconds. "The name is *Lexi*, not *princess*," I snapped, dropping my headlamp on the seat next to me. "You're lucky none of the law enforcement guys have gotten here yet. I might just have you arrested."

"On what charge?" He sounded only vaguely interested.

Since I really didn't *know* what charge, I just responded with another glare.

"Are you just going to give me mean looks or can we get a move on?" he asked, still in that tone that spoke of little to no concern about whatever answer I might offer.

I was going to regret this.

I knew it.

But I also knew that he intended to continue his search whether I was with him or not. At least if I was with him, I could use the drive time to convince him we should hook up with the others.

I wasn't about to let a civilian wander around my park at night alone. Settling back in the plush, padded leather seat, I crossed my arms over my chest. "Let's go."

He threw the truck back into drive as he drawled, "Sure thing, princess."

I didn't let myself respond, although I really, *really* wanted to.

I SPENT the next twenty minutes explaining why we were better off hooking up with my team.

Several of the other groups had already peeled off the convoy of vehicles, parking at various trailheads along the way. My team was to be one of the ones closest to the mountain, and I kept an eye on the truck that held Rafe and the SAR volunteer. When they pulled off the road at an area just wide enough for the vehicle, I pointed them out. "You can just park behind them."

But he kept on driving. "We're not stopping," he said when I swung my head around to look at him.

"I thought I'd explained this," I said, my voice tight.

"Oh, you explained plenty, princess, and everything you said made perfect sense. But it seems to me that if we want to cover more ground, we should spread out more."

"*Don't* call me *princess*," I growled at him.

I thought I caught sight of his lips twitching in amusement, and I told myself to stop reacting to his needling. It so wasn't worth it, especially since it looked like I amused him.

I eyed the road in front of us and asked, "How much farther do you plan on going? We don't want to spread ourselves too thin. Kind of ruins the point of fanning out."

"I'm stopping here," he said, guiding the truck over to the oversized shoulder and parking.

There were only so many places where one could put a vehicle if a trailhead wasn't in the area.

I made a guess at how far he'd driven and decided we were probably in a good position. As he turned off the engine, I pulled out my radio and put in a call to Rafe. His voice crackled over the line. "We're getting ready to head out, Lex. Where are you?"

"I'm not going to be joining up with you after all," I said, hoping Hailey wasn't listening.

"Is everything okay?" Rafe asked, sounding concerned.

"Good enough," I lied. "You got this, right?"

"Oh, yeah. We'll be good. Be safe."

I hadn't even had the chance to stow my radio before Roman had opened the door and hopped out, going to the small rear door on his side of the truck.

He had his pack in place before I even managed to wrest mine out.

He gave me an impatient look as I slung my pack into place. I stared him down, refusing to let him rush me as I shifted and tugged until I had my pack settled.

"Can we go now, princess?"

EIGHT

ROMAN

I DID IT JUST TO SEE HOW SHE REACTED. ALTHOUGH HER eyes flashed at me, she gave me a bright smile that once more had me shoving down the instinctive, immediate attraction I'd felt for her.

She cut around me as I settled my headlamp into place.

She was already halfway across the road by the time I had it how I wanted. I flipped it on as I crossed the road, shooting a quick look up at the sky. I couldn't make out much with the snow, but from what I could tell, the weather wasn't getting any worse.

I hoped the luck would hold, although nothing short of a blizzard would keep me from looking for Cass.

I should have made her wait a few days until a seat opened on one of the bigger airlines. It would have been safer for her.

Guilt swamped me and tried to take over, but I wrestled it under control. I couldn't afford any distractions.

The cute blonde in front of me was already distraction

enough. We'd had to go to single file as the unmarked, less traveled trail narrowed. We were already starting to climb upward, and she moved with an easy, casual grace.

We moved in silence, and although she wasn't moving as fast as I'd like, I knew the pace she'd set for us was both safe and effective.

She paused from time to time to consult the handheld GPS she carried, and impatience gnawed at me, although I understood her caution. I was sort of wishing I'd just headed straight to the trail without bothering to check with anybody else. It wasn't the most practical of ideas, and I knew we were making good time despite the crappy weather, but impatience nagged at me, making me wish I was on my own, so I could move faster.

When she stopped for the third time in under thirty minutes, my temper snapped, and I moved up until I was crowding the small space of the trail. "What's the matter, princess?" I snapped. "Lost in the woods already?"

She gave me a pithy look. "Please."

That was all she said before she looked back at the GPS, a scowl puckering her brow.

"What's wrong?" I demanded.

"Nothing's wrong," she said coolly, unaffected by the sharp tone of my voice. "I'm debating options."

I craned my head around, trying to see the screen better.

She angled it my way, and I studied the display until I saw the mark pinpointing our location. "I'm trying to figure out the best route. This one…" she tapped the screen with her pinkie finger, indicating the trail I'd planned to take, "goes almost straight up. It's a shorter distance, but a hard climb and the weather will have made it worse."

"Don't think you can handle it?"

She once more lifted her gaze to mine, and the soft gray of her eyes shone with confidence. "I'm more worried about *you*," she said with a smug grin.

I ignored the jab and focused back on the terrain mapped out on the GPS. "Where are the other teams?"

She reached into her pocket and pulled out a pen, using the tip to indicate a couple of spots on the map.

"It looks to me like the other trail will be pretty close to the next group. We won't be covering as much territory if we take that route."

She blew out a rough breath, then looked back at me. She angled her head so that the headlamp she wore wasn't shining directly in my face. I'd automatically tilted my headlamp to keep from blinding her with the bright light, but there was enough ambient light from the combined lamps that I could see her face easily.

"I'm not kidding. That trail is rough. Are you sure you can handle it?"

"I'm not the one who keeps stopping to take breathers," I drawled, although she hadn't once shown any sign of exertion. The pack she carried was packed full, and if her attitude was anything to go by, she had the smarts to know what was necessary. If she was carrying the typical gear for a search and rescue, her pack probably weighed about thirty pounds, but she didn't act like it encumbered her at all.

Still, I couldn't resist needling her.

She didn't rise to the bait though. She gave her bag one shift, then turned away, once more facing the trails. "Let's go."

ONE PROBLEM WITH THE HEADLAMP — it illuminated the excellent curve of her butt as she slowly made her way up the trail. Even those ugly uniform pants she wore couldn't hide the sheer perfection of her ass.

We'd been ascending at a steady pace for the past thirty minutes, and I was just now starting to breathe heavy. When she stopped on one of her GPS checks, I could see that her respirations were a little accelerated, and a light sweat glinted on her brow, but overall, she looked like she was taking a leisurely walk.

She pulled something from one of the webbed pockets, and I watched as she pulled out a canteen, taking a sip from it. "Did you bring water?" she asked.

In response, I lifted the tube connected to the bladder of water inside my pack. Staring at her, I took a quick swig and said, "You probably aren't drinking enough. If you do enough of these, you should get a CamelBak pack like this one."

"I'll take that into consideration," she replied in a snide tone.

As she turned away, I found myself grinning at her back. I wiped the expression off my face as soon as I noticed, giving myself a mental slap. I didn't need to be appreciating how cheeky she was, or how little I seemed to intimidate her. I was used to intimidating people. It wasn't just my height or physique either. I had a few scars left by shrapnel and one long thin one on my face that seemed to catch the attention of everybody I met.

Her ranger buddy back at the park had certainly noticed

it. What had she called him? Stilwell. What the hell kind of name was *Stilwell*? One that fit the annoying prick, that was for certain.

Lexi didn't even seem to notice the scar though. I hadn't once caught her staring at it.

I frowned at her back, annoyed by how much she was preoccupying my thoughts. I needed to be focused on the search, on finding Cass, not admiring the curve of her ass or enjoying her acerbic humor.

We walked another twenty or thirty minutes before she reached into the webbed pocket of her backpack, slowing to a stop as she took another drink of water.

"That guy back at the ranger station," I said, waiting for her eyes to meet mine.

"There were a lot of guys at the station," she pointed out. "You're a guy. You were there."

"Smart ass." I braced my hands on my hips. "The one who called you Alex. What's his deal?"

"He's an asshole," she replied simply. "That might explain why you keep calling me *princess*."

She delivered that last comment with a dazzling smile, and I found myself laughing.

Her eyes widened in surprise.

The laughter broke off, and I cleared my throat. "I call you princess because you act like one," I replied. "All prim and proper. That's not why he calls you *Alex*."

"He does it to annoy me," she said, shaking her head. She looked away but not before I caught a flicker of something in her eyes.

Something sad.

It bothered me enough that I fell silent as she turned to resume her trek up the mountain.

I'd lost track of how long we'd been out here and tugged up the sleeve of my coat to check my watch. In the span it took me to check the time, the snowfall intensified, and I glanced up just in time to catch a face full of flakes.

"Shit," Lexi muttered, looking up just as I did. I caught sight of her face in profile as she looked around and her expression was acutely annoyed. "This is going to make things so much more fun."

I grunted in agreement and nodded to the trail. "We should get moving."

NINE
LEXI

I was glad I'd added my gaiter. It kept snow from sneaking in the scant space between my coat's collar and my neck. If this kept up, my outer layer would be wet pretty quickly, but both my coat and the trousers I wore were water repellant, and my base layer should do the job of keeping me warm enough.

That didn't mean I was *warm*. I just wasn't going to be in any danger of frostbite.

I gave a brief thought to Roman and whether he was wearing a base layer but brushed the concern aside.

If he was as experienced as he'd led me to believe, he wouldn't be so stupid to be out here in just jeans and a battered leather coat. Of course, I couldn't be too critical. I'd ended up going with *him* instead of my team, something that could end up causing me problems with both my boss and the various SAR volunteers who'd come out to help.

Stilwell, that asshole, would probably start cackling with glee when he realized what I'd done.

Fuck, I'd been so stupid agreeing to come out here with Roman.

But at the same time, I tried to figure out what the other options were. Going out solo on a night like this here in the mountains was like the height of stupidity, and if something happened to Roman on his dogged search for the downed plane, then we'd be looking at not one rescue op, but two.

It was enough to give me a headache, and the man's arrogance was pushing my already frayed temper to the limits.

The trail we were following had a bifurcation coming up, and I pulled out my GPS to give it another check, coming to a halt as I did so. My thighs were burning already from the steady upward climb we'd been making, but I tuned it out of my mind. If we kept in the general direction, it was only going to get worse.

As I debated on the right path to take, I pulled my canteen from the pocket on my bag and took a drink. It was almost empty. I had several more bottles of water stowed in my pack, enough to get me through a day out here in the mountains, easy, even with all the physical exertion. Even when the bottled water ran out, I had both a small personal water filter and purification tablets, and there was an abundance of water coming down around us in the form of snowflakes. But the fact that I was almost on empty with the canteen was proof of how long we'd been out here.

I didn't check the time.

There wasn't much point.

I had my radio on and was listening to the low hum of chatter, but as of yet, they hadn't found the crash site or any survivors. Time was crucial at this point, so we'd be out here for as long as it took to find the survivors or until the weather completely shut us down.

Brooding, I studied the GPS and the two alternative routes as Roman stood next to me. From the corner of my eye, I could see him moving the tube into place, so he could take a drink from the CamelBak water pack. His backpack was a rugged, camouflaged piece of work, one designed for military use. I'd recognized the style once I had a chance to look at it and decided I needed to get one. I'd seen the CamelBak packs before, but this was the first chance I'd had to witness just how ingenious the design was.

"What's the holdup?" he asked after a few moments of silence.

I didn't even look up at him. He'd moved close enough that he could see the map on the handheld GPS easily, and I suspected he was already aware that we needed to pick a direction in the next few hundred yards. "Trying to weigh options," I said shortly.

He tapped the map and said, "We need to keep going north."

I made a face. *North* meant leaving the measly trail for one that was used even less.

I didn't like the idea.

"It makes just as much sense to shift toward the north-west," I said, uneasy about the idea of taking the less-traveled game trail. It went on for several miles before joining up with yet another trail that was close to one of the less-used ranger stations, but those few miles would be rough, and the snowy terrain would make everything more difficult than it already was.

"We go north," Roman said, tone implacable.

I was about to tell him off when he cut around me. The trail fork was just a couple hundred feet ahead according to my GPS, and as I hit the button to put the screen to sleep, I could see him striding on. I had no doubt he was heading in the exact direction I *didn't* want to go. Which meant I'd have to follow him.

It wasn't like I could *force* him to take the route I preferred. Somebody a little less arrogant or unsure would be easier to talk into taking the other route, but none of those descriptors applied to Roman.

Jack-ass.

I heaved out a breath and started onward.

We reached the spot where the trail split and Roman paused, looking around us with a gaze that was both assessing and annoyed.

"You're about to take us on what is little more than a game trail," I told him. "It's unmarked, and hardly anybody uses it, not even us rangers."

He gave me a cutting glance. "What's the matter? Don't think you can handle it?"

I flipped him off, the gesture seeming to happen almost on its own, without any input from my consciousness.

To my surprise, the corner of his mouth tugged up in a faint grin.

"Sweetheart," he drawled. He scanned me from head to toe, and I'd swear I felt *every* inch as he looked up and down.

Instinctive heat rushed through me, only to be obliterated as he added, "You only wish."

"You're an arrogant piece of work," I said in a disinterested tone, although my pride had been stung. I wasn't particularly vain, but I'd never lacked for male interest either. That he could look at me that way was an insult more cutting than I liked. "What makes you think I *would* wish?"

I cut around him, refusing to continue trailing along at his back like some undesired train.

I could only faintly hear him falling into place behind me, and I had the feeling I'd amused him yet again.

Jack-ass.

He could kiss my overly sore ass.

I can't say if my irritation was enough to cause my distraction or if I could attribute it to weather, or just the overall surroundings in general. I'd been trying to watch where I stepped while keeping an eye on the terrain around me. At the back of my mind, I knew I needed to keep alert for certain dangers, not all of which were caused by nature. Some of them were directly related to the presence of the man in the rugged mountain landscape.

But I did get distracted, and it happened all too easily despite the fact that I was continually scanning the terrain.

One minute I was moving to traverse a huge limb that was bigger around than my waist. It must have fallen only recently, the fresh wood easy to make out even in the dim light.

I jumped up on it and went to step down, and faster than I could process, I was thrown off balance, pain shooting through my ankle. Instinctively, I threw myself to the side and flung out my left hand in an instinctive move-ment to break my fall as the snare clamped its jaws closed around my foot.

I cried out as I hit, the impact jolting and not just because almost all my weight was centered on two points of contact, my left wrist and hip, while the trap around my left ankle wrenched in the opposite direction.

Bright, blinding pain tore through me, and another pained cry escaped me as I rolled onto my back, instinctively cradling my injured wrist.

Blood roared in my ears as I stared up at the sky, snowflakes drifting down to land gently on my face. Previously, I'd been too cold to take much notice of the fat, fluffy flakes as they made contact with my skin.

But now my blood was pumping hard enough that I was sweating despite the cold, and each snowflake was a small, icy burn on my flesh.

A shadow fell over me, and it took my shock-flooded mind a few seconds to place just who owned the big, hulking form that came between me and my view of the snowy sky.

Roman said something, and I closed my eyes with a groan, cradling my left forearm. My wrist *screamed* in agony.

I squirmed around, all but rendered helpless by the heavy pack and the pain in my wrist. With my uninjured hand, I fumbled free of the waist and sternum straps of my pack, but I couldn't do anything about the shoulder straps in this position except shrug out of them, and the thought of moving my left arm filled me with dread.

Roman said something else, voice sharp and commanding.

I blinked, wheeling my head around to focus on his face. My headlamp lit up his rugged features mercilessly. For some odd reason, my brain locked on the beauty of his pale green eyes, and I stared into them as if they alone could keep me grounded.

"Help me sit up," I said.

He ignored me. "Are you hurt?"

It seemed like a stupid question.

I'd stepped into a hunter's snare, and my ankle throbbed dully while my wrist hurt more than I'd thought it was even *possible* to hurt.

My voice was surprisingly steady as I said, "I think I might have broken my wrist."

TEN

ROMAN

"WE GO NORTH."

Her pretty little mouth tightened, and I could already see an argument forming in her eyes.

I could have presented my case in a logical manner, but that mouth kept distracting me, so instead of explaining my rationale, I just focused my attention on the map displayed on her handheld GPS. It was a make I was familiar with, although handheld GPS units, for the most part, worked about the same.

I wasn't as familiar with this area, and logic dictated that I use caution, but the longer we were out here without any sign of the plane, or Cass, the more concerned I became.

I could see the skepticism in her eyes, but I already knew it wouldn't affect me.

Maybe I should feel bad I was all but dragging her along with me. One part of me insisted that she hadn't had to follow me, but there was another part of me that understood her rationale.

It could be dangerous on these trails, even in daylight with good weather. We were hiking it in the very opposite, a dark, cloudy night as snow fell steadily from the skies. It was already accumulating on the ground, and that would make our going much more treacherous.

"You're about to take us on what is little more than a game trail," she said in a hard voice. There was a world of concern in her eyes and her tone.

Maybe I should slow things down and consider what she was telling me. But even as she continued to speak, the worry in my gut swelled yet again.

"It's unmarked, and hardly anybody uses it, not even us rangers," Lexi said, her voice flat and emotionless.

She was probably right. I really should slow things down and think. But Lexi's all too logical, all too rational tone rubbed me the wrong way, and I couldn't even explain why.

In an effort to cut her off, I gave her a dismissive look. "What's the matter? Don't think you can handle it?"

She flipped me off.

Heat punched through me, a sudden, heavy surge of lust – stronger than I'd felt in a long, long time.

Despite my distraction, I found myself grinning at her.

Fuck you, her eyes said.

I raked her up and down with a look. "Sweetheart, you only wish."

I said it more to get a rise out of her than anything else, but instead, she gave me a cool look. "You're an arrogant piece of work. What makes you think I *would* wish?"

Her cute little nose practically turned up in the air before she cut around me to continue on the trail.

I fell into step behind her, oddly content to do just that.

Her head was never still, something I'd already noticed. I knew from experience that she was taking in everything around her and keeping a close eye out for potential hazards. She was likely watching for any possible sign of the crash or survivors, although I sure as hell hoped the survivors stayed together. Although there had been only a couple of people on the small plane, they'd be safer if they didn't split up.

In front of me, Lexi went to climb over a heavy limb that was blocking the game trail.

Her cry, sharp and loud, caught me off guard. In front of me, she started to sway, then she went down. She went down hard enough that I heard her collision with the ground, and another sharp, pained cry echoed in the air.

I swore, climbing over the tree limb to see what happened.

"What happened?" I demanded, although the snare around her lower leg made that obvious.

Her lashes fluttered, but I could tell just by her expression she hadn't heard me.

"Are you hurt?"

All she did was groan.

Crouching down next to her, I looked her up and down. When my gaze landed on her left wrist, I immediately swore. It was already swollen. I squeezed my eyes tightly shut for a few seconds, then continued my quick visual exam. I'd gone through combat medic training as a Ranger, so before I did anything to help, I needed to get an idea of what had happened and where she hurt.

The *what* became obvious, almost immediately. Around

her ankle was a snare. She must have triggered it when she went over the downed limb.

She blinked the snow from her eyes as I shifted my attention to her face.

She squinted a little, and I adjusted the headlamp, so it wasn't shining directly into her eyes. She drew a deep, ragged breath. "Help me sit up," she ordered.

Not happening just yet, princess. I didn't say it out loud, continuing to look her over. *The* bright light of my headlamp showed that her pupils were dilated, so large that only a thin rim of gray showed around the edges.

Fuck. If she went into shock…

She still hadn't answered me, and I reached out to tap her cheek. Before I made contact, she spoke, her voice slow and level, almost eerily so. "I think I might have broken my wrist."

Don't be broken. The thought was a plea and a demand.

"Okay," I said, refusing to let anything show in my voice. "I'll take a look at it."

She squeezed her eyes shut. "I don't know if I want you doing that."

"I had medic training in the army. I know what I'm doing," I told her.

"Can you help me sit up? This isn't the most comfortable position," she said, the words tight with pain.

"In a minute. First, I need to get this snare off and then check to make sure you don't have any other injuries."

Moving to her feet, I found the mechanism to release the damn trap. It pissed me off just looking at it, but I didn't have time to think about illegal hunters right then. I just needed to be grateful that the snare had closed around her boot and not the more vulnerable pants above it. It could have been much worse.

"Ready?"

She nodded, and I pushed the mechanism to unlock the jaws. Lexi offered a sharp intake of breath as the trap released, then breathed out in obvious relief. I tossed the damn thing to the side.

"Other than your wrist, can you move everything okay?"

She took a deep breath, then began to flex and bend. When she rotated her left ankle, a strangled noise escaped her, and her lashes flew open, pain contorting her features.

"Left ankle," she said. "It hurts."

"How bad?"

She squinted up at me, and I had a feeling she wanted to deliver a sharp retort, but none came. "Hard to say," she commented after a few more seconds. "It's nothing like my wrist though. My ankle is somewhere in the range of *ouch* and *hurts like a mother-fucker,* and my wrist has blown the *mother-fucker* stage out of the water."

"Okay. So you probably didn't break your ankle. That's good." I shrugged out of my pack, then eased her into an upright position. "We can't take that pack off until we stabilize your wrist, okay?"

She nodded jerkily.

Unzipping one of the big outer pockets, I got the first aid kit and put it off to the side where I could reach it easily. I closed my hands around her lower leg and began to prod the area. When I was able to do that without hurting her, I had Lexi move her ankle again. She could do it, but it was obvious it pained her. "Your ankle is probably just sprained. I'll wrap it up in a minute."

The snow had started to come down harder in the past little while, making a bad situation even worse.

I shouldn't have pushed Lexi into coming with me. Yeah, I needed to find Cass, but I would have been fine out on my own. If I'd just gone out to search by myself, then Lexi wouldn't be lying there in pain.

Pushing the thought aside, I took her wrist and held it gingerly above the area where it was swelling. "We need to stabilize this in case it is broken."

"I know." She sucked in a breath. "Go ahead and do it. I've got a first aid kit in my pack.

"I've already got mine out." After getting out the needed supplies, I eyed the sleeve of her coat, trying to figure out how we could do this. Finally, I decided I'd just wrap her up, coat and all. It was too cold for me to cut the material away. It was even more important now to keep her warm. The splinting material that I'd carried with me as a Ranger was tucked away in the corner of the pack, and I pulled it out, tearing open the plastic wrap before unrolling the flexible aluminum material. I held it to her forearm to get an idea of how long to cut the strip, then used the utility shears in the pack. She whimpered as I put the brace into place, then folded and tucked away the material of her coat so that it added another layer of support. Once I had it taped into place, I studied her face. "Holding up okay there, princess?"

Her mouth twisted in a scowl. "You're an ass, you know that, Roman?"

"Guilty. Is the support tight enough? Think it's stable?"

"I've never broken a bone before," she replied sourly. "I don't have much to compare it to."

"You're making this real easy, you know that, Lexi?"

She made a face at me, then tipped her head back, lifting her face to the snow.

"I'm going to wrap your ankle now, okay?"

She just nodded.

Guilt tore jagged claws into me as I eased the leg of her pants up, trying to eyeball the injury. I couldn't make out any swelling and decided the boots, which went up over her ankle, had probably provided enough support to protect from any major injury. If possible, though, I needed her upright and moving. If I had to, I could make an emergency stretcher, but that would slow us down, which wasn't optional.

"I'm going to take your boot off. We should wrap your ankle."

"Fine," she said through gritted teeth.

There was a fine line between her brows, and I had no doubt she was hurting. I hated to cause her more pain, but expediency was crucial now.

The snow was coming down even heavier than before, and every moment she sat on the cold ground, it sapped more of her body heat away.

By the time I had her ankle wrapped, there was a fine sweat on her brow despite the cold, and I knew that as careful as I'd been, I'd hurt her. I unlaced her boot all the way, allowing the needed extra room now required due to her wrapped ankle.

A couple of times, she hissed under her breath, but for the most part, she was quiet.

"Okay," I said. "I'm done."

She was still pale, breathing shallowly, but at the sound of my voice, she opened her eyes and nodded.

"We're going to have to find somewhere to put up a shelter," I said, already skimming the area and trying to gauge the best location.

"Help me stand up," she said.

"You need to–"

She fixed a dark glare on me. "What I *need* to do is get my head examined for coming out here like this. Will you just shut up and listen to me instead of trying to give me orders?"

I set my jaw, then maneuvered into place, keeping my body on her left so I could brace her when the pain got to be too much. Once she realized how much it hurt to put weight on that ankle, she'd stop arguing.

But she didn't have any such realization.

She shrugged free of me and hobbled forward one small step at a time. After she'd moved about four feet, she looked back at me. "There's an old ranger station not too far from here. We need to backtrack a bit." She looked around with a frown, searching for something.

I saw what it was just as she located it – the handheld GPS. She took a step toward it. I snagged it off the ground and turned it over before she could take another step.

Stubborn woman.

"Thank you," she said, surprising me.

I fumbled with a response, but she wasn't even looking at me. Snowflakes laced through her hair, the ponytail falling over her shoulder as she bent her head to study the screen. She went to lift her left hand and immediately stopped, a hiss of pain escaping her. She awkwardly fumbled with it until she could use her thumb on the screen.

When she looked back at me, there was relief in her

eyes. "We just need to backtrack about fifty feet, then take the old trail that leads to the station."

"Can you handle it?" I asked.

She gave me a resolute nod. "If we can find some sort of limb I can use…"

"I'll deal with it." I went to the downed tree branch and studied it. Briefly, the snare caught my attention, and I scowled. I was pretty sure things hadn't changed that much since I'd been here – hunting and trapping weren't legal in this area. Whoever had placed this here was responsible for Lexi's injury. Or partly responsible. We could share the blame.

I didn't let myself brood over it just then, though. I needed to get Lexi someplace safe where she could get warm, and I could see about calling for help. I had no doubt that we'd be here overnight at least, and I wanted her out of the weather before I worried about that call.

I found the length of limb I needed and once more raided my pack, pulling out a small handheld saw. It looked like a length of chain with paracord loops on each end, and it made quick work of the branch I'd decided to cut off. In just a couple of minutes, I had a decent length of wood she could use to support and balance herself.

I turned to find her leaning against a tree, eyes closed.

She opened them when she heard me coming and looked at the makeshift walking stick. She eyed it critically, then nodded, pushing off the tree. I reached her just as she went to shift her weight gingerly onto her injured ankle. Pushing the stick into her hand, I waited close by to see how she did.

She squared her shoulders and met my eyes. "Let's get a move on."

IT TOOK FAR TOO long to get to the ranger's cabin.

She was shivering just slightly, although sweat still beaded her forehead. She needed some food and water and a fire. Once inside the cabin, I took a look around while she hobbled over to the nearest flat surface, carefully sitting down on the small, utilitarian couch.

There was a small wood fireplace, and I was relieved to see a supply of logs nearby. There were no other rooms, just the one open space that held the couch where Lexi was sitting as she freed the releases on her backpack, also a bed, a table with two chairs and the very basics as far as the kitchen went. There was no electricity from what I could tell, but that didn't matter. I had a small, collapsible camp stove in my pack and suspected Lexi did too.

I looked back over at her to see her trying to ease her way out of the backpack's shoulder straps.

"Let me help," I said, moving over to her.

We worked her right arm free easy enough, then I pulled the pack around, holding it steady as she used her right hand to push the strap down and over her splinted wrist.

She breathed a sigh of relief as I lowered it to the ground, although she tensed back up as I hunkered down in front of her. "How are you?"

"Sore. Tired. Hungry."

"Alright." I nodded and rose, slipping out of my pack

and placing it near the door. "Do you know if it's safe to light a fire?"

"Yes. The cabin isn't used anymore, but maintenance is done as needed so the place is ready to use in the event of an emergency." She blew out a breath. "I never expected *me* to be the one needing to use this place."

"I'm sorry," I said gruffly.

She looked at me, then looked away. "This is just as much my fault as yours. I could have just let you be stupid and go out on your own."

"You aren't the kind to do that." I'd figured that out within minutes of meeting her. I'd known if I headed out, she'd follow or find some other method of keeping me safe.

She opened her mouth to comment, then stopped, shaking her head. "I'm cold. Can you deal with the fire or do I need to?"

"Might be hard with a possible wrist fracture," I told her.

She flipped me off. I couldn't hide my amusement, although it felt wrong to be smiling at a time like this, when she was hurting and cold and hungry. Just the thought of that was enough to make my smile fade. Turning away, I went to the fire.

Get this place warm – that was my first priority. After it was warm enough, she could get out of her coat, and I could do a better job splinting her arm.

It didn't take long to get a fire started, using the fire starter and kit from my pack. I waited until I was sure it wouldn't go out, then rose, unzipping my coat and shrugging out of it.

There was still a bite to the air, but I'd dealt with worse, and the coat was wet. I dragged a chair over to the hearth and put my coat on the back, angling it so the heat from the fire could help it dry.

That done, I faced Lexi.

"What do you have to eat?"

She made a face. "A few MREs, some energy bars, protein powder, ramen noodles, a couple packs of dried eggs, and some instant soup."

I eyed her, then slid my gaze to the pack she'd been hauling around for the past couple of hours. "Water?"

"A few more liters in my pack, plus a water filter and water purification tablets," she responded. "I've also got some painkillers in my first aid kit – which I need."

I dug them out and turned them over to her, grabbing her canteen as well.

As she washed them down, I considered her options. I had mostly MREs and some powdered mix for protein shakes.

"How about I cook the eggs and soup for you? You need something hot in your belly."

She shrugged, the gesture listless, and I could tell the pain was wearing her down.

"Mind if I get into your pack to get the food?"

"Go ahead," she said as she squirmed her way more fully onto the couch, still babying her injured wrist.

Again, I wanted to kick myself for landing her in this mess. I also wanted to find the asshole who'd put the snare down, although the likelihood of finding him was small to none.

Still, I whiled away a few minutes, pondering what I'd like to do to the person responsible. Maybe break his wrist and his ankle, so he'd have some understanding of what Lexi was going through. Sure, her ankle was probably just sprained, but there was nothing like driving a point home.

Hunkering down in front of her pack, I unzipped it and wasn't at all surprised to find it neatly organized. She told me where to look for the food, and I pulled out the packets for the soup and eggs. There was a small metal pot with the package of Ramen noodles stowed inside. I needed the pot for the soup, so I put the noodles aside and added the pot to my stash.

Lexi's radio crackled.

I looked up as she pulled it free from her collar and listened.

Relief punched me hard as a man's voice came over the line.

"Update. The crash site has been located, and there are no fatalities. Several non-emergency injuries were sustained. Teams have already been sent out to bring the survivors in where they'll be transported for medical care. All other teams should report back in with location and ETA."

Feeling like a burden had been lifted off my shoulders, I let myself relax just a fraction. My relief was short lived, crashing down to nothingness as Lexi held the radio to her lips.

"This is Ranger Lexi Evers..."

Her voice remained calm and professional as she informed the command center of her injury and location, but I could see the tension brewing inside her. It grew only worse when she was asked where her team was, and she informed them she hadn't gone out with the team. By the time she was done explaining the situation, she'd become so rigid I thought she might break at the lightest touch.

There was a long silence after she finished talking.

Finally, a male voice came on the radio. "Ranger Evers, this is Hawthorne. I've received your location and am aware of your situation. Are you secure for the night?"

"Yes, sir." She was staring hard at one of the small windows, although there wasn't much to see but snow and the darkness of night.

"The weather is getting worse so if you can hold out for the night, we'll send a team to collect you in the morning."

"Understood, sir. Thank you." She started to lower the radio, but it crackled again, and she lifted it back up.

"Don't go thanking me right now. This is a mess you've landed in, Evers."

"I understand, sir."

The radio went silent, and she lowered the handset to the couch and covered her face with her good hand. Trying to give her some privacy, I turned away from her and focused on getting her some food ready.

A sly, sharp voice in the back of my head murmured that I wasn't being truthful.

But I hadn't ever been very good at lying to myself. I wasn't trying to give her privacy – I was trying to hide from her. Well, hide the best I could considering we were both trapped in a small cabin not much bigger than some bedrooms.

Long, taut moments passed with neither of us speaking. I got her food ready and took it to her, then dug an MRE out of my pack. Meals-ready-to-eat weren't exactly fine cuisine, but I had no desire to do anything but fill the hole in my belly, and the basic fare would do just fine.

"You can have some of the eggs and soup if you want," Lexi said.

I shot her a look, but she had her attention on the eggs I'd mixed up then served to her on a small plate that had been part of her mess kit. She shoveled up a bite, then sipped soup from the canteen cup.

"This works for me," I said, going through the familiar motions of preparing the MRE.

"Suit yourself."

Another silence fell, and I tried to pretend I was alone, although I didn't really succeed. I gave up trying when Lexi moved, then gasped out, clearly in pain.

I was at her side in seconds. "What is it? Are you okay?"

"I'm fine," she said, her tone aggravated. "I was just trying to move a little, and I put too much weight on my ankle."

"Can I help?"

She shook her head, glancing at me out of the corner of her eye. "I'm good right now."

I couldn't really insist so I went back to the food I'd been preparing.

"You don't have to sit on the floor," she said in a dry tone. "I'm pretty sure I'm not contagious."

But she was. The wry smile in her voice tugged a response from me, one I smothered and locked down. Her fiery temper called to me, as did the confident way she had handled herself throughout the night.

At her second chiding comment, I gave in and went to sit on the couch at her side, although I didn't let myself look at her. I kept my attention on my food, eating it without really tasting anything.

"You looked relieved about the news on the crash," she said, putting the small plate down. She'd completely cleaned it.

"Yeah. You want something else to eat?"

"No. I'm good. Can you help me with my coat?"

I should have already offered. It was nice and warm here on the couch which sat close to the fireplace. The farther corners were likely still chilly, but that would soon abate.

She dragged the zipper down awkwardly. My gaze strayed to her hand, but I immediately redirected it, looking elsewhere. Then she grumbled under her breath, and I swung my gaze around to see that the zipper had caught.

I was being punished.

I knew it.

My mouth was dry as I lifted my hands. "May I…?"

"Please." Her voice was surly, but I understood. I'd been injured to the point that even the most basic, simple tasks required aid.

I kept my gaze focused on the task at hand, working the zipper free with far more care than the chore probably needed. I didn't ease up on my focus, though. If I stayed on task, I wouldn't be tempted to look into her eyes.

That temptation faded away to nothing as I eased the sleeve on her right arm, then went to work on her injured side. I had to remove the splint, and I knew once that protective support was gone, it would be that much easier to cause her more pain.

She was breathing hard when I finished but hadn't made a sound. I checked her expression, and although that fine line was once more between her brows, she didn't look too uncomfortable.

"Thank you," she said.

Our eyes met.

Tension once more pulsed in the air, the kind I hadn't felt in ages. Her pupils spiked, and I knew I wasn't the only one who'd just felt that immediate, demanding tug. I tried to ignore it, focusing on Lexi and her injuries, not Lexi and her sexy mouth.

I re-splinted her wrist and forearm, telling myself not to notice the soft smoothness of her skin, or how good she smelled.

"Let's get your boots off. I want to check out your ankle and wrap it better. I couldn't see for shit out there."

Her eyes fell away, and she nodded. But when she went to lift her leg, I caught her foot. "I'll do it. Easier for me since my hand isn't hurt."

I half-expected her to argue, but she didn't. I tugged the laces free on her uninjured foot first, then moved to the other one. The ankle was definitely swollen, but when I rotated it one way, then the other, her response was nothing more than a grimace.

"I don't think anything is broken here," I said, rewrapping the ankle. I pushed the leg of her pants up, so I could take the wrap a bit higher and couldn't help but notice the elegance and strength of her calf. It took more restraint than I liked to admit to not stroke my fingers down her skin.

Once I was done, I sat down to finish my food, careful not to look at Lexi.

"Who was on the plane?"

Immediately, I tensed but forced myself to relax. Certain

events in my past had caused me to become even more guarded than normal, and I'd always been a private person anyway. Now it was worse, and I had no desire to discuss personal matters with the very sexy ranger sitting just a few feet away. In an effort to deflect her question, I hitched up my shoulder and kept my attention on my rapidly diminishing meal.

Lexi was determined, though, and continued to subtly prod and nudge me for information.

Surging off the couch, I collected everything we'd used for the meal. Refuse was never left behind out in the wilderness. It just invited trouble – various kinds of trouble, for certain, but trouble nonetheless.

After Lexi made another reference to the crash, I turned around and snapped, "Why the hell are you so nosy?"

"It's called *making conversation*," she replied, her chin going up slightly. "It's not like we've got a lot of ways to pass the time."

I must have lost my mind.

That was the only explanation for what happened next.

"I disagree," I said as I closed the distance between us and bent over the couch. Her eyes widened as I caught her slightly pointed chin in my hand and slammed my mouth down over hers.

I WAS HALLUCINATING.

Delirium, maybe, brought on by the unending ache in my wrist and ankle. Or maybe I'd hit my head when I fell, and the blow had knocked me out, and I was dreaming.

That might explain why Roman was *kissing* me.

Yes, he was hot, but we'd been sniping at each other almost from the get-go – and when he wasn't sniping at me, he was just trying to antagonize me. Not exactly the set-up for a lip-lock.

But unless I was dreaming…

Maybe I was. This was definitely better than the self-satisfaction I'd been forced to indulge in lately. So…I'd enjoy it. He stroked his tongue along my lower lip, and I opened wider, unconsciously reaching for him. The second my left hand touched his shoulder, pain flared. Any attempt to convince myself this was a dream fell apart.

I jerked back, starbursts going off behind my eyes as my

injured wrist made a very demanding protest in response to my action.

Roman stared at me, eyes intense, a pure, pale green that was oddly beautiful, almost soft compared to the harsh lines of his face.

He dropped his gaze to study the hand I cradled against my chest.

"Maybe use the other hand," he suggested. Then he kissed me again.

A breath caught in my throat, and before I could manage to free it, he knocked it right out of me as he deepened the kiss. Everything inside me turned to molten, hot flame.

I'd learned my lesson, so this time when I kissed him, I kept my bad arm cradled carefully against my chest as I reached for him with my good one. Twining it around his neck, I tugged him closer.

He complied, going to his knees in front of me, both of his hands now cradling my face. His touch was gentle, so gentle, another oddity in a world now filled with them.

Kissing never felt like this. Not for me at least.

This kiss wasn't just a prelude to whatever might happen next. It was an entire experience in and of itself. He made a low noise in his throat, hungry and demanding. The sound of it made my nipples peak and harden, and I whimpered. Need and dismay tangled, then rose inside me.

Some part of my brain was stuttering in shock. *I... what...you can't...*

But the rest of me was already shouting, *Go for it, Lexi.*

His mouth left mine to cruise down my neck, and I angled my head back to grant him better access. He rewarded me by raking his teeth down the exposed arch, sending a shiver through me.

That stuttering part of my brain tried again. *You don't know this guy. What are you doing?*

No. I didn't know him. But other than the nagging voice of common sense, nothing in me seemed to *care*.

I knew how his mouth felt on mine – *amazing*.

I knew how he tasted – *amazing*.

And then he placed a deft hand on my side, slipping it under my shirt and gliding upward until he cupped my breast.

Now I knew how his touch felt – *amazing*.

It didn't matter if I knew this guy or not. I was already all in. I couldn't even think of the last time somebody's touch had lit me up like this, and I didn't want to miss a second.

When he slid his hand back out from under my shirt, I whimpered in displeasure, only to sigh as I felt him tugging at the buttons of my shirt. He pulled back as he freed the first one, watching me. He moved onto the second, and I bit my lip.

"Am I stopping?" he asked, voice gruff.

Mute, I shook my head, falling back to brace my weight on my good hand to give him easier access to the buttons. I still had my wrist cradled against my waist, and as he drew closer, I had to shift it out of the way.

Even that slight movement had the pain flaring. I tried to hide it, but he saw anyway.

"Come on," he said.

Before I could figure out what he meant, he had me in

his arms and was carrying me across the floor of the small cabin.

He moved like I weighed *nothing*. I knew for a fact that I wasn't a lightweight. I wasn't vain, but I knew I had a good figure. Staying in shape was important for my job, and I took it seriously. I was also curvy – almost voluptuous, a fact that had embarrassed me when I had to start wearing a 36D bra by my sophomore year. Boobs were the bane of existence when a girl was a tomboy.

But he moved with ease, and my head started to spin just a little as he laid me down on the bed.

He carefully caught my arm at the elbow, guiding my injured wrist up over my head. Then he went back to dealing with the buttons of my dull, tan uniform.

Suddenly, I wished I was wearing something more appealing than the utilitarian black bra and panties I'd pulled on earlier that morning. I found myself wondering if I'd remembered to shave and how sweaty had I gotten during the long, cold hike.

Then, after freeing the last button, Roman spread my shirt opened and all those thoughts died. The look in his eyes was so intense, so hot, I wouldn't have been surprised to find myself burned. He freed the front clasp of my bra and nudged the cups open. I stared at his face, afraid to even blink for fear that I'd wake up and realize that I'd been wrong – this *was* a dream.

But deep inside, I knew it wasn't.

I couldn't dream up something as erotic as this. I couldn't imagine how amazing a simple finger could feel as he traced a path along my skin up to circle my nipple.

"Your tits are beautiful," he said.

The blunt statement made me blush – and squirm. I'd only ever had one lover, and that had been years ago, and he definitely was *not* the type for dirty talk. I'd never really given it much consideration, though. They were just words.

But I'd have to re-evaluate my stance, because hearing those words come from Roman was enough to have an arrow of heat lancing through me and centering between my thighs.

He bent over me, and I gasped, bringing my good hand up to twine through his hair as he took my nipple in his mouth. The heat was searing and shocking and completely divine. I moaned and arched closer.

He worked an arm beneath me, bringing my lower body in flush against his as he came down between my thighs.

Now I was moaning for a whole new reason – the rigid, heavy length pressing against me in the most intimate way imaginable. Okay, maybe not the *most* intimate. But the second most.

He pumped his hips against me, sending my panties, already damp, sliding back and forth over my clitoris.

"More," I begged, rocking against him as best as I could, considering I was pinned under the solid mass of his body.

His response was to pull away completely, and I stared at him in dismay.

But then he whipped his shirt off. For a moment, the sight of his bared chest stunned me into silence.

He was a work of muscle, sinew and taut, tanned skin – and scars. There was a thick length of one carving down from his shoulder. Another one on the left of his navel. Other small ones peppered his torso, and instinctively, I wanted to run my hands over each one and soothe any aches that might linger.

Then he was back over me, and I felt the shocking heat of his body pressed against me, skin to skin, from the waist up. I shuddered. Shoving a hand into his hair, I hauled his mouth back to mine.

He came easily enough, and I lost myself in his kiss yet again.

But that wasn't enough for long, and I found myself arching and rubbing and clinging.

He shifted his weight, and I gasped as he opened my pants and slid them down my hips before sliding a hand between my thighs, pressing down against me with the heel of his hand. My clitoris practically stood up and applauded at the attention. My entire body went taut and stiff as all my being focused on him, on his touch and the way he skillfully worked me.

When his hand left me, I wanted to scream in frustration. Then his fingers were there, inside my panties, and I could do nothing but arch into the sensation.

He groaned as he touched me, muttering against my mouth, "Fuck, Lexi. You're so wet."

I knew I was. I could feel it as he circled his fingers around my clit before stroking down lower. One long finger arrowed into me, and I all but shrieked with need as he began to pump that finger in and out, a slow, steady rhythm that drove me higher and higher.

His lips pressed to my ear. "I want to taste you. Tell me I can."

"Yes." I didn't even fully understand what I was giving him permission to do, but whatever it was, I wanted it.

In the span of seconds, he'd levered himself off me and had my pants down to my ankles. He slowed a bit as he eased them off, taking care of the sturdy wrapping on my left leg, but then as soon as the pants were off, he flung them into the recesses of the cabin. I tensed as he spread out between my thighs, his mouth on level with the apex of my thighs.

A strangled cry escaped me as he pressed his mouth to my cunt.

He wasn't deterred.

He increased the pressure, mouth closing around my clitoris. Then he started to suck.

Once more, starbursts exploded behind my closed lids, but it was because of pleasure this time, not pain…so much better. I pushed my free hand into his hair without thinking, pressing him closer.

He didn't need the urging though.

As I was still whimpering from the first initial contact, he shifted positions and pushed two fingers inside me, twisting them as he thrust them deep.

The orgasm hit me too hard, too fast, knocking me off guard as I arched under him.

A low, rough noise escaped me, one that defied definition, but I was too caught up in sensation to even puzzle it out.

He paused, lifting his head to shoot me a quick look.

"More," I said, a plea in my voice.

He gave me a wide, wicked smile then pressed his mouth back to me, a hot, open kiss against my pussy.

I went to bring up my legs, maybe in an effort to bring him in closer, but he caught my left one, resting his hand on my knee. Without even looking at me, he muttered, "Careful. Don't want you hurting yourself."

Hurting?

What in the hell could hurt right now? Except maybe him stopping. But he was soon back to working me with both mouth and tongue, and I totally forgot about pain of any kind...except the slow, sensual torture he inflicted with his mouth and tongue.

He worked me right back to the edge, then left me teetering on the brink as he rose and stared at me where I lay splayed out and open for him. If I could have thought clearly, I might have considered closing my legs. I didn't do vulnerable, and this was about as vulnerable as a woman could get.

But I was more interested in watching him as he tugged his wallet out and withdrew a condom.

A wisecrack instinctively leaped to my lips, brought on by a sudden spate of nervousness as he placed the foil packet between his teeth, then lowered his hands to the button of his jeans. Through sheer willpower alone, I kept it behind my teeth, which was just as well. My mouth started to water, and by the time he had his zipper down, the nerves had been replaced by greed.

He tore the condom open, and I stared raptly as he unrolled it down the heavy length of his cock, then gave it one final tug before bending back over me, settling his knees between my spread thighs.

His weight was hot and startling, the feel of all those muscled and angled planes feeling utterly alien.

The one lover I'd been with had felt nothing like this.

He pushed his hand into my hair, and I stared at him,

entranced as he slowly twined the thick, silky mass around his fingers. "Your hair is beautiful."

I might have said thank you, but then I felt him nudging against my entrance, and my lashes fluttered shut.

He lifted one hand to my neck, using his thumb to nudge my chin up. "Look at me, Lexi."

I couldn't disobey that rough command, and I lifted my lids to find his intense gaze locked on my face.

"That's better. I want to see your eyes as I fuck you."

My breathing hitched, and I realized there *was* a more vulnerable position for a woman to be in. It was this one, with a man's cock pressing against her folds, demanding entrance while he stared as if memorizing every last expression, from her ragged breaths to her startled cries.

One of those startled cries ripped out of me as he flexed his hips and thrust deep, seating himself inside me with one hard lunge.

I went to grab at him. He gently caught my injured wrist. There was a twinge of pain, but it was lost in the erotic sensation of having him stretch me. With my good hand, I clung to his bicep, gasping as he withdrew, then filled me again, just as hard, just as deep, just as fast.

It went straight to my head, and I knew without a doubt if he kept this pace up, I'd very shortly be shivering and moaning as I came around him.

As if he sensed that very thing, he adjusted his rhythm and moved higher on my body, his thrusts going slow, almost torturously so. I sank my short nails into his arm and lifted up, trying to goad him back into that sweet, fast pace.

But he kept it slow, even pushing up onto his hands and staring at me as he rocked against me.

He shifted one hand up over my shoulder, smoothing the other one down until he could cup my breast in his hand. He rolled the aching nipple back and forth between his finger and thumb, stopping from time to time to tug on me. That light pull of his fingers arrowed right through me and echoed down in my pussy, forcing me to contract around him.

That was the first sign that this was having the same sort of effect on him. He closed his eyes.

In echo of his earlier comment, I said, "Look at me...I want to see you."

The thick fringe of his lashes lifted. A muscle pulsed in his jaw, and he thrust harder into the cradle of my hips.

I arched up with a ragged moan, and he dropped his weight back down on me, shoving one hand down to palm my ass. He lifted me up, changing the angle of my lower body and the next thrust had him pressing right against my clit.

Another one of those unfamiliar, foreign sounds escaped me, part moan, part cry, all need.

He moved faster and was soon back to the driving rhythm that had so delighted me only moments ago. His cock throbbed as it rasped over sensitive tissues, and I whimpered as I felt my climax raging closer.

He saw it too. I could tell just by looking in his eyes. Hot, sexual male hunger gleamed down at me, and it only added to the sheer eroticism.

I came, hoarsely crying his name out.

He slammed his mouth down on mine and drank the noise down, while against me, his long, powerful body shuddered. He thrust inside me once more, then held there.

I felt the pulsations of his cock jerking within me and knew he was coming too.

As he sank down to rest his head against my chest, he muttered something under his breath.

It was my name.

TWELVE

ROMAN

I WAS A COLOSSAL IDIOT.

That was the most-polite phrase I'd come up with to describe my actions over the past hour. I'd cursed myself in every language I knew, then started all over again in English, the self-directed anger becoming more and more intense as the minutes ticked by into hours.

Lexi lay sleeping on the bed, huddled under the blankets, with just the tip of her toes peeking out. She had all but wrapped herself in the covers, cocooning herself in their warmth.

I wanted to go back to her and curve my body up behind hers, sharing my heat.

But I'd already done one incredibly stupid thing.

I didn't need to compound it by cuddling with her.

The logical part of me kept demanding answers. *What had I been thinking? Had I lost my mind?*

I had no real response to those internal questions, other

than the fact that I hadn't wanted to talk about the plane or about Cass, and giving into the strange, sudden attraction I'd felt for her almost from the get-go had been one hell of a diversion tactic.

It had worked a little too well, though, because I'd let myself get distracted as well.

By the time I'd freed myself from the tangle we'd made of the blankets, Lexi had been asleep, and the fire had started to burn down. We'd need the fire for its warmth, so I'd been able to busy myself with the simple task of adding more logs and waiting for them to catch flame before retreating back to the couch. It was the only place to sit save for one of the hard, ladder-back chairs at the table, and as pissed off as I was at myself, I wasn't about to subject my sore ass to that kind of punishment.

Across the room from me, Lexi sighed and rolled over onto her left side. A sharp noise escaped her, and her lids fluttered, lines fanning out from her mouth as if in pain. She must have bumped her wrist or her ankle.

I watched another moment to make sure she wasn't going to wake up, then I slumped back into the couch cushions and pondered what had happened.

It had been years since I'd been with a woman. Guilt and a need for self-isolation had pushed things like sex over to the wayside.

For a long while, I'd completely lost interest in sex. The mess in my head and memories haunting me had made it easy for me to compartmentalize a lot of things, relying on just the necessary actions to get through, each and every new day.

Sex, to my surprise, hadn't been as necessary as I'd once thought.

Unless that was sex with Lexi.

I had a bad feeling she was like heroin – one taste and I was addicted. I wanted so much more than what we'd had, and that was something that wasn't going to happen.

There were too many things in the way, and even if there weren't, I didn't deserve a woman like Lexi.

Even after only a few hours in her presence, I'd come to understand certain things about her. She was strong, determined and resourceful. She didn't bellyache over the little things, and she'd handled even the big things without panicking – getting caught in a trapper's illegal snare had to count as big.

She sighed in her sleep, and I shifted my attention back to her just in time to see a faint smile curl her lips.

Resisting the urge to return to the bed and tug her up against me, I wondered just what it was that had such a sly little smile curling her lips while she slept.

"You've got to stop this shit," I told myself, rising and stalking over to the window.

The snow that had hampered our search had finally started to lessen. It looked like there were a few inches of the fluffy white stuff on the ground. It wasn't anything that would prevent some sure-footed, experienced hikers from hitting the trails if there was a need for it, but with Lexi's swollen ankle and likely broken wrist, I couldn't call her sure-footed. Not now, at least.

She *had* been, moving through the forest with an ease and confidence that spoke of somebody who'd been doing it for a long while.

The only thing I could take comfort in was the fact that despite her fall and the pain in her ankle, she likely only had a sprain and that would heal. She could go rest up and heal, then easily return to her ranger job here in the Rockies.

Of course, that was assuming she didn't end up in trouble for aiding me.

Even more than ever, I now wished I'd just gone on by myself. She wasn't just stranded and injured in a small ranger's cabin, several miles from the rest of her group, she could be looking at disciplinary action of some sort.

I had no idea how a forest ranger unit operated, but I did know that some forest rangers were commissioned peace officers, which made them law enforcement. Any time it came to law enforcement, there were procedures to be followed, and shit could ensue if those procedures were ignored. I'd likely screwed with her career on top of getting her injured.

And it hadn't even been necessary.

One of the other rescue teams had found Cass.

My mind drifted toward her. Was she hurt? They'd said there were no fatalities, but that didn't mean there hadn't been serious injuries. The thought of it was enough to clear my mind of the problems I'd likely caused Lexi, and my thoughts shifted to worry.

Cass would be okay, I told myself.

She *had* to be. I wasn't about to lose anybody else.

I'd known her for so long.

She was a part of my life, shitty as it was. The only decent part I could claim anymore.

I DOZED off and on during the night, slumped on the couch and never really letting myself fully relax. It was because of this that I woke at the first sound coming from somewhere outside the cabin – it was a noise that didn't belong. Years of living with my back to the wall, wary that death could come at any minute had sharpened my survival skills, and I was on my feet, immediately trying to place whatever had woken me.

It took a few more seconds for the noise to come again, and this time, I recognized it.

Somebody – or bodies – were approaching the cabin.

I glanced outside to see that it was past dawn, although still a little dim under the heavy growth of trees.

Although I knew it was likely the rescue team coming for Lexi, I waited at the window until I caught sight of the familiar, drab uniforms.

I turned to her and woke her up, glad I'd had her put on her clothes before going to sleep.

That was the last thing she needed, the harassment that could come if any of her co-workers realized what had been going on in here during the night hours.

She was sitting on the edge of the bed, her hair rumpled but eyes surprisingly alert given I'd just woken her from a sound sleep. She shoved a hand through her unkempt hair, attempting to tame it. It helped a little, but she still had that sexy, disheveled thing going on. I wanted to go to her and kiss her one last time, but even as I contemplated it, there was a hard knock on the door.

I heard the *click* sound of a lock, and in seconds, four other park rangers were inside the cabin.

One of them was the asshole from last night, and he gave me a sidelong look that he probably didn't intend for me to see before focusing his attention on Lexi.

"Alex, you went and caused an awful lot of trouble," he said, voice domineering. "What were you thinking, violating procedure like that?"

She lifted her head slowly and pinned a look on the man that would have made a wise man duck for cover. "Shove it, Stilwell," she said in a cool voice.

"Stilwell, Lexi, we'll discuss this once we're out of here and Lexi has a chance to get her injuries evaluated," a tall, broad man said as he moved to crouch in front of Lexi.

"Sir, I–"

"Stilwell, you heard me."

The obnoxious ass fell silent, and I studied him from between narrowed eyes.

Stilwell.

Last night, I recalled thinking how *Stilwell* sounded like an asshole's name. He'd done nothing but confirm my suspicion that he was, in fact, an asshole.

"Stilwell." I crossed my arms over my chest and stared at him until he shifted his gaze my way. "Aren't you the wise guy who told me that she could help me out and get me to the crash site?"

He sputtered for a moment, his jaw working up and down. "I never *meant* for her to bring you out here. You're a civilian–"

"Let me quote something you said to me last night..." I cut him off, getting more and more pissed. This fuck-up was partly responsible for Lexi being out here. If he hadn't pointed her – or anybody – out, I would have gone solo.

"You said, *'This guy says he's the one who rented the plane that went down. He wants to join in with the search group. I told him you'd be the best bet to take him out to the crash site.'*"

His eyes darted to the man kneeling in front of Lexi who had paused in the process of unwrapping her ankle. That man gave me an appraising look before focusing back on the job at hand. Guess he decided either it wasn't worth trying to rebuke *me*...or he wanted to hear what I had to say.

"I hardly *meant* for Lexi to go off half-cocked with an untrained civilian—"

"I'm not a *civilian*," I said, cutting him off again. "I'm an Army Ranger and can probably handle these woods and anything the weather can throw at me better than half you boys."

Stilwell stiffened in insult, but before he could say anything else, I continued. "And if you didn't *intend for her to go off half-cocked*, then why did you point her out to me in the first place and tell me, quoting again, *'She'll help you out. If you're that determined to go out, maybe she can take you to the crash site.'*" Memorizing details, down to the most minor ones was necessary for a Ranger, and my near-eidetic memory had come in handy more than once. I didn't just remember things I'd *seen*, but things I'd heard, even years before. Giving Stilwell a sharp-edged smile, I added, "You also gave me her name, although the wrong one. Is any of this ringing any bells?"

Stilwell's face had gone an ugly, mottled shade of red.

In a calm voice, the man who seemed to be in charge said, "Stilwell, why don't you go outside and help get the basket ready?"

Stilwell didn't reply, just turned on his heel and stormed out.

Lexi's eyes drifted my way, and I managed to offer her a faint smile. She smiled back, and I thought I saw relief in her eyes.

The look was quickly gone as the man looked between the two of us, giving me an appraising look before focusing back on Lexi. "Pretty ugly sprain," he said, taking her heel. "Let's see how well you can move it."

Lexi grimaced and let him gingerly prod and work at her ankle.

"I doubt anything's broken," he said finally. "You need to get an X-ray to make sure."

"Yeah, I know."

He shifted his attention to her wrist, and she curled her other hand around her injured arm. "You're *not* messing with my wrist, Hawthorne. There's some deformity so I can pretty much guarantee that it's broken."

The ranger, Hawthorne, nodded. "Well, I guess you went and paid the price for not following procedure."

She scowled at him, and he shook his head.

A noise from the door had us all looking in that direction, and I watched as Stilwell and another ranger brought in a basket stretcher. I'd seen them before, back when I'd still been an active Army Ranger and had even had the unfortunate honor to be transported out in a similar contraption when I'd been injured in a hostile area.

The black metal contraption had a concave surface area that would cradle and protect Lexi as they transported her out of here, as well as straps to help secure her in place.

If we weren't in such a heavily wooded area, they might

have air-lifted her out, but the dense tree coverage made that impossible.

Lexi gave the basket a look of acute dislike, but she allowed Hawthorne to help her stand, supporting her on her injured side so she could use his body as a crutch and keep weight off her ankle.

Once she was on the stretcher, Hawthorne put the safety straps in place, then moved to the head. Stilwell started for the end of the stretcher, but one of the other rangers beat him to it.

"Stilwell, make sure the cabin is secure," Hawthorne said as they carried Lexi out.

I didn't trust the jackass to do a decent job of it, so I made sure the fire was out. That left him to collect the bag of trash left over from the night before. In that moment, I was glad I'd made sure to tie the bag shut, sealing away evidence of the condom I used last night.

Stilwell gave me a sly look and glanced at the bed. "I guess you two ended up getting pretty cozy during the night, didn't you? Alex is a hot piece of ass, so if things got a little heated, I can't say I blame you."

"Stilwell," I said, shaking my head. He passed by me, and I shot out a hand, grabbing the stiff, upright collar of his winter coat. Jerking him close, I stared into his face, not bothering to hide the anger burning in me. "First...she goes by *Lexi*, not *Alex*. Second, if you even think about going off and running your mouth, I'm going to knock your teeth down your throat."

Then, with a rough shove, I pushed him out of my face and headed out of the cabin.

They were still loading Lexi onto what looked like a

rugged little golf cart with an extended bed designed for carrying equipment, or in this case, a patient.

Stilwell headed for the front of the vehicle, his face an angry red.

"I'm driving her back, Stilwell," Hawthorne said, not even looking back at him. He gave me a quick look and jerked his head toward the cart. "You'll be riding up front with me. Anders, you stay in the back with Lexi. The rest of you are hoofing it out of here."

From the corner of my eye, I saw Stilwell's face go ugly and mottled, but the expression faded fast, and he flashed his boss a quick smile. "You sure you want to try navigating the trail with the utility cart, boss? It's been a while since you were out in the field."

Hawthorne looked at Stilwell, and something in his eyes made me think he didn't much care for the bastard either. They finished securing Lexi and the stretcher, and he hopped down out of the back of the cart with fluid agility. "I think I can handle it, son, but I appreciate the concern."

He said it in such a way that the words came off in a polite, subtle rebuke.

I could tell by the look on Stilwell's face he had heard it as well.

I strolled past the asshole and gave him a grim smile. "Have a nice walk back."

ONCE THEY GOT Lexi back to the ranger station that had served as last night's staging area, I asked what hospital Cass had been taken to.

Hawthorne told me, and I gave him my thanks.

"You can thank me by never trying to drag one of my people out onto the mountain with you. If you want to be involved with a search, be a volunteer."

"I had somebody on that plane, sir," I told him with a shake of my head. "I couldn't just sit around. But I don't plan on forcing my way into anything like last night any time soon."

"Good." Hawthorne turned to Lexi as the paramedics went to transfer her out of the basket.

I could have easily left at that point but found myself lingering for reasons I didn't entirely understand.

"Lexi, I'll drive your car back to your place and have Anders follow me, so he can get me back out here. It will probably be a little later in the day, but I expect you'll be at the hospital for a while." Hawthorne stood close to Lexi, but I could still hear them as I hovered there, waiting for what, I didn't really know.

"Thank you," she said.

He narrowed his eyes at her and added, "We'll discuss your actions once you're back on your feet, got it?"

I heard the warning in his words and eyed Lexi as she swallowed, then offered a nod. "Yes, sir."

She was loaded into the ambulance, and I overheard the paramedic mention the name of the hospital. It was the same one they'd taken Cass to.

I WAS COMING up on Estes Park when my phone started vibrating, letting me know I had messages. Hitting the play button on my car, I listened to them via the Bluetooth link.

Several were from Cass, two were from her mother. I deleted them after I finished listening. I sent Cass a quick message.

On my way to see you at the hospital.

Then I checked the screen to see if I'd missed any calls.

I most definitely had – like seven of them. I glanced once more at the screen then redirected my attention to the road. It had been a while since I'd been to Estes Park, but I knew where the hospital was and made my way there, mostly on autopilot, my thoughts returning to the events of the past fifteen hours.

How much had I screwed things up for Lexi?

I had no idea, and it was possible I wouldn't ever know, but I knew I'd caused her problems, even aside from her injuries.

Shit.

I hoped that bastard Stilwell didn't make things any worse for her. Briefly, I thought about calling the park and seeing if I could talk to Hawthorne, but I decided against it. I couldn't tell him much more than he'd already heard, and I had no doubt he'd be talking to Lexi soon. Maybe once he realized it hadn't been carelessness that caused her to get hurt, but the snare, it would help Lexi out.

I got to the hospital in record time and was directed to where I could find Cass.

I found her lying in a bed, her eyes closed. There was a dark bruise forming on her cheek and a small bandage at her temple. Her right arm was in a sling. Her wrist protruded in a cast.

I didn't make a sound, but she heard me anyway, opening a pair of beautiful blue-green eyes. They filled with relief at the sight of me, and she held a hand out to me.

I went to her immediately, some of the tension I'd been carrying finally starting to fade away. Moving toward her, I caught her hand in mine and summoned up a reassuring smile. "Hey, sweetheart."

I HAD A MINOR ANKLE SPRAIN AND A BROKEN WRIST THAT WAS
going to require surgery to set. That was just my luck. The
doctor advised me that my ankle would likely heal within
one to two weeks, but the recovery time for my wrist would
be easier to determine after they'd set the bone.

Unfortunately, they couldn't get me into the operating
room until the next morning, which meant I had to stay
overnight.

This was just my luck, and I put in a call to update
Hawthorne after the nurses told me I'd be transported to my
room as soon as they had one ready.

I felt like an invalid laying in the bed, and there was
nothing to do to distract myself. I didn't have any of my
stuff, save for my phone, and it was rather difficult to do
much with it since I only had the use of one hand.

An IV bag hung on a pole next to me, some sort of
steroidal medication being fed into my body via the tube.
They'd also given me some pain medication, and I could

feel the heavy weight of it affecting each of my muscles. My head was spinning more than a little, so I closed my eyes.

I woke up to find myself being wheeled down a hallway. I rubbed at my tired eyes and looked around as we passed by several closed doors.

"Good morning, sleepyhead," a cheerful voice said.

I craned my head around and saw a grinning man in scrubs. He slowed the gurney to a halt outside one of the open doors. He said something, but a familiar voice caught my attention, and I looked across the hall into the other room. My heart lurched at the sight of Roman sitting on a bed with a woman. Neither of them saw me. The woman, a cute brunette, leaned against him, and he wrapped his arm around her as he told her he'd take care of it – whatever *it* was.

I averted my eyes as the uniformed hospital worker started to turn the gurney and ease me into the room right across the hall from where I'd seen Roman.

Great. Just great.

I wondered who the woman was, although it wasn't likely I'd ever ask.

For all I knew, I wouldn't see Roman again after this. Ever.

The thought caused my heart to pang.

———

THE EFFECTS of the painkillers were still clouding my mind, and not long after I'd been transferred out of the gurney and into the bed, I fell asleep.

I came awake at the sound of a knock on the door.

At first, I could only make out a fuzzy shape, and I rubbed at my eyes in an attempt to clear them. It had to be the medication.

"Hey, Alex! How are you feeling?"

This time when I looked at the visitor, I could see him much more clearly. Why in the hell did I have to wake up?

Stilwell approached me and leaned over the bed, looking me over. "You look rough," he said in a tone that oozed false sympathy.

"Gee, and here I was thinking I was about ready to win a beauty pageant," I said sarcastically. My filter was pretty much disengaged at that point, but I didn't know if it was because of the medication, the pain, or just my general exhaustion.

Stilwell's brows shot up. "Ouch."

I stared at him, and I had no doubt my eyes conveyed my displeasure at seeing him there.

He smoothed a hand down the front of his shirt and said, "I need to get a report from the people involved in the plane crash, but I wanted to come by and say hi while I was here."

I bared my teeth at him in a sharp smile. "How considerate of you."

"Have you talked to your new buddy any since you got here?"

"My new buddy?"

"Aw, come on. Don't tell me you forgot his name already. Roman, right?" He tugged something from his breast pocket and displayed it for me. "They make a cute couple, don't they?"

I stared at the picture, hard, not quite believing what I was seeing.

It was Roman...and the woman he'd been sitting with when I'd seen him earlier. They both looked young and happy as they smiled at each other. She all but glowed, which I guess was fitting since she was wearing a wedding dress.

A *wedding* dress.

The son of a bitch was *married*.

I didn't let my reaction show, just shifted my gaze back up to Stilwell's face. "Maybe he's *your* buddy, seeing as how you've got a picture of him."

"Oh, no. I found this back at the cabin," he said easily. "When I was locking everything down, I caught sight of it on the floor, all but hidden under the bed. I guess he dropped it. I was hoping to return it to him."

"How kind of you." I closed my eyes and averted my face. "I'm tired now, Stilwell. Why don't you get to work on collecting your reports?"

He lingered a moment longer, but then I heard the soles of his clunky uniform shoes striking the floor as he left the room.

I couldn't even be relieved that he was gone, though.

I was too busy thinking about that picture.

Roman and the nameless woman, smiling on their wedding day.

Men really, *really* sucked.

I WAS ONCE AGAIN AWOKEN by a knock on the door.

The pain meds must have been wearing off because I was starting to hurt again – and I was forced to squint for the next thirty seconds as I waited for my vision to clear.

A tall man with graying hair and glasses came in, clad in scrubs. He had an engaging grin on his face as he came to a stop by my bed. "Sorry to wake you, Ms. Evers. I'm the orthopedic surgeon who'll be taking care of you in the morning."

"Hello," I said. My mouth was incredibly dry, and I reached for the cup of water on the wheeled, over-the-bed table without thinking about my hand.

"Here," the doctor said. "Let me get that."

He circled around the bed and passed me the water, and as I took a sip, he brought the table around so that it was on the right side of the bed. "Thank you."

"Of course. I'm Dr. York, by the way. I came by to see if you had any questions for me."

I glanced at my splinted wrist, then shot him a look. "Is there any chance of permanent damage?"

"Not likely." He shook his head, his blue eyes bright with intelligence behind the shield of his glasses. "This is a relatively simple procedure, and you're young. We're lucky that it's a closed fracture. Had it been an open fracture where bone protruded through the skin, there's always the risk of infection. Especially since you weren't able to get in the night it happened. Once we get the bones set, the pain will go away, and you can go home after you spend a few hours in recovery."

"Okay." I frowned, trying to think if there was anything else I should ask.

A knock at the door interrupted my thought process.

Everything inside me chilled at the sight of Roman.

He stood there, just inside the door, eyes roaming over me, cataloging every feature, from my head to the splint on my wrist down to my legs, although they were hidden from view by the blanket. Once his gaze returned to mine, I said coolly, "Go away, Roman."

Then I focused back on the doctor. "Once my ankle heals up, I should be able to go back to work, even with the cast, right?"

FOURTEEN
ROMAN

THE COLD LOOK IN LEXI'S EYES AS SHE DISMISSED ME STUCK with me as I stood in the room across the hall. Cass was listening to the nurse as she went over discharge instructions, and I tried my best to focus on that conversation, but my mind kept returning to Lexi.

Why was she so pissed at me?

But even as I asked myself that question, I had to swallow back a humorless laugh. I'd all but dragged her out into the snow where she got hurt by a trapping snare. She was likely facing disciplinary action from her boss, and she was in the hospital.

Why *wouldn't* she be pissed at me?

"…Roman?"

I jerked my head up and focused on Cass. She looked tired, but she was still a beautiful woman. I shook my head. "I'm sorry, my thoughts were wandering. I didn't hear the question?"

Cass rolled her eyes and gave me an affectionate smile. "I was asking if you had any questions for the nurse."

"No. I'm good." Glancing at the nurse, I asked, "Should I go ahead and bring my truck around, so I can take her home?"

"Absolutely." The nurse smiled at me. "One of the volunteers is already on their way with a wheelchair."

Cass wrinkled her nose. "Can't I just walk?"

"Sorry." The nurse shook her head. "Hospital policy. If you don't have any more questions, I'll be on my way."

"I think we're good," Cass said.

After the nurse left, I went to grab the folder the nurse had given Cass. "They give you anything for pain?"

"Yes. The prescription is in there." She nodded at the folder I held. "We can get it filled on the way back to my house. I can't drive for the next twenty-four hours because of the painkillers they've given me."

"If you're too tired, I can take you home and go back out for it."

"No. I want it filled so that if I start hurting, I have something to take." She offered a faint smile. "You know how much of a baby I am."

"You were in a plane crash less than a day ago, and you're sitting there smiling. I don't think you qualify for *baby* status anymore, honey."

I HELPED Cass out of the truck. I was parked in the street right in front of the house where she lived with her parents.

She'd moved back in with them as their health started to decline so she could help them out.

"You sure you don't want me coming back out here to stay the night in case you need help?" I asked as we walked to the front door.

"I'll be fine," she said, voice chiding. "You should go home and get some rest. You look worn out."

The front door opened, and Cass's mother came out, moving with more speed than normal, her cane tapping the floor as she moved across the porch. "Cass," she said, her voice breaking.

Cass moved to her mother and caught the frail older woman in a one-armed hug. "I'm fine, Mama," she said softly. "I'm fine."

I stood there uncomfortably as the two women spoke, ready to get out of here and get back to my place. I had too much restless energy and the self-directed anger I'd been shoving down ever since Lexi had gotten hurt wasn't helping.

I felt like I was going to explode.

But I kept my hands in my pockets and nodded politely at Mrs. Debion when she finally pulled back from Cass and faced me.

"Thank you *so* much, Roman," she said, voice steadier now and oddly strong considering how frail she'd become over the past few years.

I followed them inside and did a walk through the house, trying to think if there was anything I should take care of before I left. Cass tried to convince me that they were all fine, but I didn't like leaving her here with only her aging parents to help if she needed anything.

Cass had followed me into the kitchen, and she got a glass down out of the cabinet and filled it with water. She gave me a sidelong look as she sipped from it. "It's going to be fun trying to be a leftie for the next few weeks, huh?"

"I just bet."

She narrowed her eyes shrewdly as she took another sip. After lowering the glass, she asked, "So, are you going to tell me about it?"

"About what?" I gave her a puzzled look.

"What has you so…" she scrunched up her face, then finished, "pissy."

"Pissy?" I echoed, slightly amused despite the ever-darkening direction of my thoughts.

"Yeah. You've got something going on, and it's bothering you."

"You *were* just in a plane crash that could have killed you," I pointed out.

"Don't remind me," she muttered. "But that's not what's bothering you. I can tell."

I had no doubt she could, but I wasn't discussing Lexi with her.

FIFTEEN
LEXI

BREANNA PARILLO DROVE LIKE A BAT OUT OF HELL.

I loved almost everything about my cousin, but I *hated* riding in a car with her. Unfortunately, unless I called one of the rangers I worked with, she was the only one I could think of to take me home after I was discharged. I was stuck with the insane driving for another fifteen minutes, then I could try to get over the trauma inflicted by her need for speed.

I clenched my teeth as she took the next corner a good fifteen miles faster than the posted speed limit.

"I've already got one broken bone, Bree. I don't need you to wreck and send me back to the hospital with even *more* broken bones."

She laughed, unperturbed. "Almost there." She shot me a look. "You look like you're hurting again. Glad we stopped and got your painkillers."

"I'm not hurting – I'm *terrified*," I told her dryly.

That just made her laugh again.

The rest of the drive passed in silence, and I blew out a breath of relief as we finally pulled into the driveway of my cute little A-frame log house. I went to work on swinging my legs out while Breanna got the odd contraption I'd been given to help me walk as I couldn't use crutches with my broken hand.

She came around the car, awkwardly fumbling with the hands-free crutch. I thought I could probably manage without the device, but the more I rested my ankle, the quicker it would heal.

Using my good hand, I gripped the side of the car and hauled myself out.

Breanna scowled. "I could have helped you."

I shrugged. "I've got to figure out how to do these things by myself."

"You're so stubborn," she said, shaking her head.

I hopped a few more inches from the car so I could put the crutch on. With my knee on the platform, my ankle was off the ground. I'd used a similar one at the hospital to see if I thought it would work and the physical therapist had instructed me on how to put it on and secure it. The bands went across the back of my thigh and around my lower leg, keeping the device snugly in place.

Blowing out a breath, I looked up at the house. "Okay," I said. "Let's do this."

Breanna shut the door then moved to my bad side, ready to help me if I stumbled. I was scared to death I would.

But after a couple of steps, I found it easier to walk, and the tension in my shoulders eased. Of course, once my gaze landed on the steps, the nerves returned. I eyed them with trepidation. There were only two of them, but they looked a lot higher than I suspected they were.

Breanna stopped next to me and slid me a look. "You're going to have to figure something out. I can't carry you."

"Ha, ha," I said, moving closer. I'd done some digging around online as we drove from the hospital to the medical supply store recommended by the physical therapist and had seen advice from fellow users. Once I got to the steps, I turned around and gripped the railing with my right hand. Then I went up backward. It was an unusual way to do it, but it worked.

Once I was on the small porch, I grinned at Breanna. "This might not totally suck after all."

She snorted. "Just wait until you have to wash your hair one-handed."

"Party pooper," I muttered. I hadn't even thought about that.

She just laughed.

I OPTED to go for sponging myself clean the first night home. I had some dry shampoo that I used on my hair. It hadn't been the perfect fix, but it had sufficed, giving me a little more time to adjust to the cast and my fancy new crutch.

But come morning, I laid on the bed with the knowledge that if I didn't get a real shower, I was going to scream.

I hadn't had one since the day I'd gotten hurt, and it was driving me nuts.

Inside the bathroom, I fumbled out of the loose nightshirt I'd pulled on the night before, then reached for my brush so I could deal with the tangles before climbing into the bathtub.

For some reason, as I watched myself drag a brush through my hair, I found myself remembering that night. Roman. His hands in my hair, his voice a raw whisper, *your hair is beautiful.*

I want to see your eyes as I fuck you.

My nipples went tight and hard, and a punch of need slammed into me.

Deliberately, I made myself recall the picture of him and his wife, smiling at each other.

That was enough to cool my suddenly overheated skin, and I finished the job of brushing my hair. Still irritated, I pulled a water proof sleeve over my cast and climbed into the shower, moving gingerly. The crutch could be worn in the shower, thankfully. It was definitely a tight fit, but I managed easily enough.

I was glad I'd gone for the tub/shower combo instead of a separate one when I was working on the house's remodel. I'd gotten the house far cheaper than one would expect, all because of some cosmetic issues that I'd fixed for under ten grand.

Sometimes, I thought of the house as the last gift I'd ever receive from my father. He'd grown up the only child of two very wealthy people. My grandparents on his side died before I ever had a chance to meet them, and they'd left their entire estate to my father.

He'd liquidated it at some point in his life before he married my mother, tucking the money away for his future children. He and Mom had always planned on having several kids, but that hadn't happened, and when I was twenty-one, I took full control of the money he'd received when he liquidated.

It was because of that money that I'd been able to go to my school of choice and get this house, all without signing a single loan.

Thoughts of my father made me melancholy, and my heart ached with missing him.

Sniffing, I turned the water on and set about getting good and clean.

Breanna called me on Saturday, offering to come up from Denver with Chinese.

"I just took one of the pain pills," I told her, wishing I had held off. But I'd knocked my broken wrist against the wall, and it had resulted in a persistent, nagging ache.

"Well, crap." She sighed heavily. "I don't want to get all the way up there, and have you fall asleep on me."

"Chances are I'd be asleep before you got even halfway here," I told her dryly. "How's that sexy man of yours?"

"Ryder is absolutely *wonderful*," she said, the delight in her voice evident over the phone. Even without looking at her, I knew that her eyes would be glowing, and she'd have a smug grin on her face.

A tug of envy shot through my chest, and I pinched the bridge of my nose, telling myself not to think that way.

I'd already figured out the dating game wasn't for me. Maybe I'd set my stakes too high, or I just had no dating savvy, but most of the guys I'd been out with had pretty much disappointed me almost from the get-go. Not *all* of them. My college boyfriend, Royce, had been pretty amazing, but at the same time, I'd known there was no future there. We'd have fun while it lasted, and once I realized how things were, I'd called it off.

An image flashed through my mind.

Roman.

Immediately, I banished it. It was almost simple, even. All I had to do was think of the picture of him and his wife.

His *wife*, the deceptive piece of shit.

"Maybe he and I can both come up tomorrow, and we can all go out to lunch," Breanna said, unaware of my distraction.

I focused back in on the conversation. "Sure. That sounds good. I'm dying to get out of the house."

EVEN THOUGH I had indeed had lunch with Ryder and Breanna the day before, come Monday morning, I was all but crawling out of my skin. I was going stir-crazy, and the only thing that would help would be getting back to my routine.

The doctor had told me I was free to return to work on Monday if my ankle wasn't hurting, and although it was still a little achy, I'd been walking without the crutch since last night.

I'd be fine as long as I didn't have to handle any sort of trail duty for the first day or two. Just in case, when I dressed, I put on an ankle brace I'd used a few years ago when I'd developed a high ankle sprain. The extra support would come in handy, and when combined with the hiking boots, I was pretty sure that even if I stepped in a snare *again*, I would get through it relatively unscathed – except for my hands of course.

I gave the cast on my left wrist a look of acute dislike as I pulled the front door shut behind me and headed for my Jeep. Hawthorne had been true to his word and brought the vehicle to my house while I'd still been in the hospital.

I hadn't heard from him since then, and that made me antsy.

I had heard the warning in his voice loud and clear when he'd advised me we'd be discussing my actions. This wasn't just going to drift away after a few days.

I had screwed up, and it was time to pay the piper.

On the drive to the park, I coerced my thoughts away from the upcoming confrontation, admiring the beauty of the country around me and thinking through the various jobs I might be assigned until they'd deemed me suitable for my regular duties.

I managed to successfully distract myself all the way to the park.

Maneuvering my Jeep into a space in the cramped lot, I took a deep breath, then gingerly lowered myself to the ground, keeping my left hand cradled against my middle so I didn't jolt or reflexively grab at something.

I bumped into a couple of fellow rangers on my way to clock in and took their ribbing with good-natured calm. Just as I went to clock in, Hawthorne appeared. "I need to talk to you, Lexi."

"Okay. Just let me clock in–"

He shook his head. "You don't need to. Come on."

Dread curled inside me, and I turned away from the computer and followed him to his small, cramped office.

He gestured to a seat. I would have preferred to stand but didn't want to argue.

Slowly, I sank down into the hard seat with its pathetic vinyl cushion.

"You need to take a few more days off," he said in a firm voice. "We're still discussing how to handle last week's incident, and until we come to a decision, you won't be allowed to work."

Panic hit. Hard. "But I–"

He shook his head. "There's no point in arguing. What you did was serious, and there will be repercussions."

I lowered my eyes and stared at my hands.

"Lexi," he said in a gentler voice.

I looked up at him reluctantly.

"I'm trying to convince the folks higher up the ladder to just give you a one-week suspension without pay. I'm hoping they'll go for it. You're young, and this is the first problem we've ever had from you. But it will be best if you just go home and wait until you hear from me, okay?"

He gave me an encouraging smile and rose. "Come on. I'll walk you out."

I'd rather he didn't, but I wasn't about to tell him.

I'd rather slip through the side door unnoticed, so nobody was aware of my current humiliated state, but as he came around the desk, I pushed myself up and gave him a polite smile.

I'd get through this with my shoulders back and head held high. Even if it killed me.

It wasn't until we were nearly at the door when I remembered something. Slowing to a halt, I looked at Hawthorne. "Were you all able to find the snare?"

"We looked," he allowed, the corners of his mouth tight. "But we didn't find one."

"It was just up the trail from the station where we stayed the night. Right past a fallen limb that was blocking a lot of the path."

"We found the limb – it's been removed." He shoved his hand through his hair as he continued. "But there wasn't any sign of a snare."

"But–"

"Three of us went out," a new voice interjected.

My spine automatically stiffened as Stilwell placed himself at my side, giving me a condescending smile.

"We looked in that area and spread out for a bit just to check." His eyes held mine, and I saw the smirk in the back of his gaze. "Are you sure there was a snare in that spot?"

I opened my mouth, then closed it.

Shifting my attention back to Hawthorne, I found him watching me with an unreadable look on his face. "The snare was *there*," I insisted.

Hawthorne just nodded. "I'll go out there with one of the guys and double-check, okay?"

It was the best I was going to get.

Ignoring Stilwell, I told Hawthorne, "Call me if you find anything, okay?"

SIXTEEN

I managed to keep a fragile hold on my temper until I was well away from the park. But by the time I reached the halfway point between the park and my place, I was about ready to explode. In a fit of anger, I gripped the steering wheel tight as I shouted, *"Fuck!"*

That didn't help much, so I just screamed, a long, wordless noise of pure anger.

Stilwell had really tried to fuck me over this time, to the point that I might end up losing my job.

There was no denying that I bore some of the blame, but if he hadn't sent Roman my way, *none* of this would have happened.

If you'd used your common sense, none of this would have happened, I reminded myself.

It was that knowledge alone that kept me from whipping the car around and speeding back to the park, so I could get in Stilwell's face. He'd had it in for me pretty much from day one. I even remembered the exact moment I realized he was out to get me. It had been right after one of the mandatory meetings, and I'd said something that Hawthorne had approved of, eliciting a rare smile from him.

Stilwell came up to me not long after that and suggested that Hawthorne and I were screwing.

I'd been disgusted at first, but then he made a move on me, and the disgust quickly became fury.

After I informed him that I'd rather have sex with a monkey than with him, he'd looked so pissed, I wouldn't have been surprised if he'd tried to hit me. *That* would have been rewarding, because I would have knocked his lights out for trying.

The asshat was probably all but drunk with delight over what he'd brought about.

But then again, maybe not.

In my mind's eye, I saw the look on his face as Roman reminded him – in front of Hawthorne – who'd suggested *I* take him out into the park. That memory made me smile, despite my persistent anger with Roman. If I *did* still have a job after this, it would be because of Roman's interference. What a bitter irony. I was only in trouble because of Roman, and yet he'd stepped in and explained the events that brought him to me that night in the park.

I felt a tug in my chest at the thought of Roman, and I sighed, now oddly melancholy. I'd never felt the sort of attraction that I'd felt toward Roman – *still* felt, to be honest.

And it was useless and pointless and pathetic, because he was married.

Talk about some shitty luck.

I SPENT most of Monday wavering between brooding and raging like a crazy woman.

By the time Monday night rolled around, I was tired and had a headache the size of Mt. Elbert. I had also moved on to the self-pity stage and decided to cope with ice cream, bourbon, and a movie marathon.

It must have helped because I didn't even remember falling asleep.

Waking up…that was a different story.

I would *definitely* remember waking up, considering I felt dog-sick and my headache was now about the size of Kilimanjaro.

After washing down some anti-inflammatories to deal with the headache, I practically crawled into the shower. My sore ankle ached a bit, but for the most part, it was no longer plaguing me. I thought briefly about going for a walk but decided to give my ankle a few more days before starting back on my regular exercise routine.

Since I couldn't sweat my headache away as I would have liked, I went to my gym and did circuits on the weight machines, pushing myself hard. It took forever since I could do little on my left side, but I did my best.

After a brief stint in the steam room, I felt almost human.

Now, after a day to think, brood, and steam over everything that had happened, I told myself I needed to figure out a way to prove what had really taken place in the forest. I needed my boss to believe that I *had* been injured due to a snare. It wouldn't change the outcome of whatever disciplinary action was taken, but there was more at stake than just my job.

There was somebody poaching in the park, and that had to be dealt with and investigated.

I didn't know why it took me so long to find the simple answer to my problem. Maybe it was because I was still in avoidance mode when it came to thoughts of Roman.

He had seen the snare.

He could back up my story.

Maybe he could do it in person, with Stilwell looking on so the bastard looked like the jackass he was for suggesting I'd made up a story about an illegal trap set in the national park.

The problem was I had no idea where he lived.

But in this day and age, some digging could turn up almost everything, so I hit the internet.

I came up with more than a few possibilities, and it took what felt like forever to eliminate them, especially since I could only guess at the proper spelling of his last name. There was *Sayer*, *Sayre*, and *Saier* to begin with. And considering there was also the possibility that he could have used only his first initial, my list grew pretty long pretty fast.

It wasn't until almost four that I decided to reach out to a friend who worked with the state police. Lauren and I had met during a search and rescue op, back when I was still in college. I'd been a newer volunteer and Lauren had been assigned as the senior member of one of the groups I'd searched with. Being the youngest of the group, she'd grouped the two of us together, and over the three-day search, we'd gotten to know each other.

I was hoping she might be able to help me out, but when I put in the call to her, it went straight to voicemail.

Despondent, I went back to my search.

I clicked away from the general search and did an image search. After fifteen or twenty pages of results netted me nothing, I went over to a news search.

It was on the second page that I lucked out.

Local area fallen Army Ranger to be honored at Memorial Day event in Lyons.

I almost didn't click on the article when I saw the ranger's name listed in the meta description – Ryan Sayer. He wasn't who I was looking for. But I figured it was unlikely to be a coincidence, so I clicked on the link.

The article was two years old, and the picture that had been published with the article was missing, that familiar red *X* in its place, signifying either that the picture had been deleted or was in the wrong directory somehow. The text for the image reads *MSG Ryan Sayer*. I skimmed the article and at the bottom found mention of a brother...Roman.

Satisfied I had more of an idea where to focus my search, I closed the article without reading any more of it.

AS IT TURNED OUT, it was easier to track down the town where Roman lived than it was to get his actual address.

There *were* no R. Sayer or Roman Sayer of Lyon, Colorado in any of the white page sites I searched.

It grated on me, but I finally found a *Cassandra Sayer* – Roman's wife.

She had a Facebook page, and I wavered about sending her a message, asking her to have her husband contact me. In the end, I didn't. I felt too awkward to even think about sending a message to the wife of the man I'd stupidly slept with just a few days earlier.

A little more digging netted me their address, but it was too late in the day to go out there.

Frustrated, I went to bed with the plan to get up early enough, so I could make the drive out to Lyons and hopefully catch Roman at home.

───

IT WAS A QUICK, easy drive and the morning was bright. After a couple of warm days, the chill had returned to the air, and there was frost on everything.

A few fat, fluffy white clouds were drifting across the sky as I pulled into a gas station just inside the town limits.

I'd slept fitfully and was guzzling caffeine to compensate. I needed both a refill on my coffee and a bathroom break because of said coffee.

I was standing in line waiting to pay when somebody came inside. Out of habit, I glanced over then away.

It only took a second for recognition to hit.

Whipping my head around in an epic double take, I watched as Cassandra Sayer approached. Unfortunately, I wasn't at all subtle about my interest in her because she noticed and eyed me curiously.

My mind went blank.

Finally, after a few more seconds, I managed to summon up my nerve. "Hi. You're Cassandra Sayer, right?"

"Yes…I go by Cass, though." She cocked her head as she studied me. "Do I know you?"

"I was one of the volunteers the night your plane went down. I was working with Roman."

"Ah." A deprecating smile curled her lips, and she glanced down at her arm, then at my wrist. "Roman mentioned that his partner had gotten hurt. I guess it was a rough night for both of us."

"Yeah." Feeling awkward, I looked away. "Actually, I'm out here hoping to speak to Roman. Is your husband at home?"

Her lids flickered. "My..." Something flashed through her eyes. Pain, I realized. Pain and sadness. "My husband?"

"Ah...yeah. Roman."

This time, her reaction had nothing to do with pain and everything to do with amusement. She broke out laughing. "Roman is *not* my husband."

Now, I was confused. "But..." I stopped, realizing how odd it would be for me to point out that I'd seen a picture of them – a *wedding* picture.

She saw the confusion and her laughter faded away, replaced by a gentle smile. "I was married to Roman's twin...Ryan. He died a few years ago."

An odd twist of emotions whirled through me. Relief but also sadness for this woman. "Ah...his twin?"

"Yes." Cass nodded, her smile dying. "He was killed on a mission. It was supposed to be his last one. He was due to re-enlist but had already decided he was leaving the army."

Wow. "Oh, I'm so sorry."

She nodded. "Thank you. I wasn't laughing at you, by the way. It's the idea of me with Roman..." She made a face. "The two of us are like brother and sister. Do you mind if I ask why you need to speak with him?"

The line around us shifted, and I moved forward to the counter, paying for my coffee before stepping back toward her.

"It's about the night we were out searching for you." Guilt bubbled in me as I thought of how I told Roman to leave me alone when he'd come to see me at the hospital. I needed to apologize.

"Okay." She pursed her lips. "But you won't find him at my place, and I have no idea if he's home or not, although he probably is."

She paid for her gas, and the two of us moved toward the big, double glass doors. I held it open for her, and we moved to the side.

"I don't suppose you could tell me where he lives, could you? I spent most of yesterday trying to track him down and thought I'd finally located him – by searching for you." Talk about a wasted day.

She grinned at me. "I can give you his address. But be warned – he's been a bear since that night. His mood is practically toxic."

I almost asked if that was a new thing, considering how acerbic he'd been when we were together, but decided I'd already stepped in it enough.

SEVENTEEN
ROMAN

EXHAUSTION HAD MY BRAIN GOING HAZY AND MY BODY NUMB as I brought the hammer down on the post in front of me.

The fence needed repair, but if I'd been smart, I would have started the chore on a day when I wasn't so exhausted.

I wasn't smart, though, because I was plugging away at the task, and after a face-cracking yawn, I brought the hammer down and hit off-center of my target...and smashed my thumb.

"*Fuck!*" I shouted. I hurled the hammer and straightened, staring at the injured digit. It was already red.

Pissed off, I kicked the post, and it creaked ominously.

That just pissed me off even more, but I managed to restrain the urge to just kick the damn post all the way down.

Turning my back, I headed up toward the house.

Inside the kitchen, I grabbed an ice pack from the freezer, then went back outside, dropping down on the porch. If I stayed inside where it was warm, I was likely to fall asleep.

Maybe I needed to do just that.

I'd been awake for more than twenty-four hours, and before that, I'd only managed to grab an hour or two of sleep. Going long periods without any decent rest was something I was used to – being a Ranger required it. But I wasn't running high on adrenaline in the middle of a clandestine op. I was just pushing myself, and after too much time without more than an hour or two of sleep, it was clouding my brain and affecting my reflexes. And my aim. Scowling, I looked down at my throbbing thumb and decided I was done working on the fence repairs for now.

Weariness beat at me, and without any conscious thought, I leaned against the nearby post and closed my eyes.

I had no intention of falling asleep.

I hadn't intended to smash my thumb though, either.

SHE WAS WHISPERING MY NAME.

I had to be dreaming, because I knew Lexi wasn't here talking to me.

She said my name again, louder, then she touched me.

I turned my face into her palm and dragged my lids up.

"You've got to get up, Roman," she said, reaching down to take my hands. "Come on, big guy. You need to get up."

"Why don't you c'mere instead?"

She shook her head. "Get *up*, Roman. Now." Her words

were urgent, and that more than anything, pierced the thick cloud of sleep.

She tugged on my hands. "Move your ass, Roman."

"You're really here," I said slowly, trying to make sense of it.

"Yeah, I'm here, and you've been outside so long, you're probably hypothermic. We need to get you inside. Stand up. I can't drag you in. You're too heavy."

I was about to argue with her, but I realized how heavy my limbs felt and the drugged-like haze of my thoughts.

I didn't feel cold, which was a bad sign.

I *should* feel cold.

It took far too much energy and concentration to simply get to my feet, and I had the humiliating thought that I might not have been able to do it without Lexi's help.

Once I was upright, she nagged, bullied, and urged me inside the house, through the kitchen and into the living room.

She nudged me back onto the couch and grabbed a blanket, threw it around my shoulders before crouching in front of me to take my boots off. "I can do that," I said. The words came out slurred and rough, almost intelligible even to me. Dimly, my brain kicked itself into gear and reminded me that the slurred speech was another bad sign.

I was most definitely hypothermic.

Once she had my boots off, she grabbed another blanket, a quilt that my mother had made not long before she died. She wrapped it around my feet and lower legs. Some part of me wasn't too keen about the fact that my mother's prized possession was now swaddling the lower half of my body, but the energy to do something about it eluded me.

Lexi was mumbling to herself, and I looked up, focusing on her, on the bright, red-gold beauty of her hair. She crouched down in front of the fireplace and in what seemed like a blink, she had a fire crackling.

She shoved a chair closer to the fire, then came over and took my hand again.

I resisted, too tired to move, but once again, she bested me when it came to the stubbornness department. I grunted in aggravation as she propelled me closer to the chair.

Once I sat down, my irritation faded, though. The warmth from the fire felt good.

She went and fetched the blankets. Soon I was tucked back in under them, and she brushed my hair out of my face. "You're a hard-ass, Roman. You know that?"

"Am I?" The idea puzzled me, but my thoughts were so fogged and weighed down, I couldn't figure out why.

My lids drooped down, and my fogged, exhausted brain went dark.

THE FAMILIAR SOUND of gunfire raged around me.

I saw a brilliant flash, the muzzle flare of an enemy weapon. Without hesitation, I aimed in the direction where the flare had been and fired. The suppressed sound of my MK Scar L hadn't even faded in the air before I heard a loud, pain-filled scream.

Shit.

Hadn't delivered a kill shot.

I moved closer, aware of the rest of my team as we closed in on the target area.

We were taking heavy fire.

From the corner of my eye, I saw one of the guys cut around the door where I'd seen the muzzle flare, and in short succession, there were two more bursts from a silenced MK Scar.

One of the guys had taken out the hostile there.

I pressed on, locked on the house in front of us, staring at it through night vision goggles as I searched for any sign this might be a trap.

I neared the far end of the block, relying on the shadows of the nearby buildings to help hide my presence.

I looked across the road, my eyes already seeking out the other half of the team. One of the men flashed me a thumbs-up and a wild grin. That grin was an echo of my own, worn by one Ryan Sayer. My twin brother and best friend was leading the secondary assault team, and once we gave the signal, the units providing support for the team would move into play.

I looked back at the target, carefully lifting my foot. Before I could put it down, the world exploded around us.

I slammed into the building at my back, knocked off my feet by the blast from the unseen IED.

Screams shredded the night air.

Hands shook me.

A voice shouted my name.

Jerking upright, I lashed out, grabbing the person in front of me. Without thinking, I moved forward, then down. I didn't stop to look or even think about what I was doing, not until I had my forearm shoved under her neck.

Her neck. Her slim, pale, fragile neck.

Lexi.

Her eyes stared up into mine, wide with shock.

I pulled my arm back and shoved upright, kneeling in front of her. Covering my face with hands that trembled, I gulped in air. I couldn't seem to catch my breath. My heart raced and raged like a freight train while blood roared in my ears.

"Hey…"

Her soft voice made me shudder.

I'd thrown her to the ground like a madman.

She brushed her fingers down my arm. The light touch made me flinch, and I practically fell on my ass in an effort to get away.

She just followed me, shifting onto her knees. She reached out, brushed her fingers down my cheek, holding her cast tight against her chest.

"You were having a nightmare," she said.

I didn't need the update. I'd had the nightmare so many times, I'd lost track.

"Do you want to talk about it?"

"No." I squeezed my eyes shut.

After a long pause, she asked, "Is there anything I can do to help?"

I looked up at her and told myself to send her away. It was the best thing, considering my frame of mind.

She inched closer. Covering her hand with mine, I reached for her with my other one, not even thinking about what I was doing.

I pulled her up against me with one rough tug, and she practically fell into my lap. Her soft, surprised cry was cut off as I covered her mouth with mine.

My head was spinning.

It had started doing that in the seconds it had taken Roman to pounce on me and trap me beneath him, and it was still doing it now as he swept inside my mouth with keen, urgent hunger.

Although I'd been terrified just seconds earlier, the rush of adrenaline flooding me now had nothing to do with fear and everything to do with pure, undiluted desire.

I curled my arms around his neck and wiggled around until I was straddling him.

He caught my waist in his hands, and I shivered, already anticipating the feel of his rough hands on my skin.

He didn't leave me to wait long, either. He tugged me in closer, then slid both of his hands upward, dragging my shirt along as he went.

He broke our kiss only long enough to finish stripping me of my top.

I whimpered as he pulled me back against him. Through

the waffle-weave material of his thermal shirt, I could feel his heat. It was hard to believe that just over an hour ago, he'd been out on the porch doing his best imitation of a human popsicle. Now he was hot and demanding and greedy.

I didn't mind a bit.

In fact, I wanted *more*, so much more.

Reaching out, I hooked my left arm around his neck, digging the fingers of my right hand into his bicep, desperate for more of his heat.

He slid his mouth along my jawline, then down. He raked his teeth down my neck, sending a shiver of sensation through me.

Big, warm hands cupped my breasts through my bra, and I pushed against him eagerly.

He pushed my bra strap down.

As he closed his mouth around one nipple, my head fell back. My bones seemed to dissolve, and I groaned. He circled my nipple with his tongue, eliciting a whimper from my throat.

He shifted, and the room spun around me as he tucked me on the floor underneath him.

My pussy clenched as he settled between my thighs, shoving himself against me. I felt the pulse of his cock, and it was enough to drive me almost insane.

He worked his way down my body, going to his knees when he encountered the barrier of my jeans. With quick, efficient movements, he dealt with both my jeans and my boots. My thighs fell open for him as he stretched out between my legs. He kissed me through the barrier of my panties. I shoved my hand into his hair and fisted it, pressing him tight against me.

I thought I just might die from the pleasure of it as he tugged the band of my panties and exposed me to his mouth. He licked me, stabbing his tongue into me, an echo of what I *really* wanted from him.

Not that I minded him going down on me – at *all*. Still clutching at his hair with my uninjured hand, I pressed him closer.

He sealed his mouth over me and kissed my cunt, the exact same way he'd kissed my lips, with devouring, devastating hunger.

I writhed under him, desperate to climax.

Just when he had me almost to the brink, he pulled back.

I stared at him and arched my hips. "Please."

"I want to be inside you when you come," he said, voice hard, tight and flat. He shoved his jeans out of the way and came over me again, reaching between us to steady his cock and aim it right at the heart of me. I cried out as he filled me, stretching me and burning me and marking me.

I wrapped my arm around his neck, trying to trap him as close as possible.

He made no attempt to put distance between us, and I shuddered in ecstasy as he thrust inside me, again and again and again.

I shuddered under the onslaught.

His lips rubbed over mine.

I opened for him, catching his lower lip between my teeth and biting him.

Roman tensed against me.

Without thinking, I did it again, sinking my teeth into his lower lip, then sucking the full lower curve into my mouth.

He shuddered. A few taut moments passed. He shoved up onto his hands, weight balanced between his upper and lower body...and centering on the connection between us.

He continued to hold still, and I opened my eyes, gazing up at him.

He caught my right knee in his hand and pushed it up, holding it flush against his hip. It deepened his possession of my body. Thrashing under him, I clung to his bicep with my good hand while scrabbling under him and working against the heavy, thick ridge of his cock.

He pulsed inside me. I was acutely aware of it, of every ridge, every jerk of his cock.

He pulled out until we were barely connected.

Then he slammed into me.

Again and again, and soon, I was shouting out his name, my voice almost hoarse.

The smooth wood of the floor scrapped against my back.

His fingers slid up and squeezed my ass.

He sank his teeth into my neck.

The climax exploded inside me.

A split second later, Roman withdrew.

Dumbfounded, I stared up at him as he pushed onto his knees and wrapped his hand around his cock.

His naked cock.

He began to pump and understanding dawned.

I was overcome with a deep, vicious urge to push his hand away and replace it with my mouth, but I was a bit compromised at the moment. I couldn't have found the strength to move if the house had burst into flame in that very moment.

So I lay there, shuddering in the aftermath and watching as he worked his cock until he came, the thick wet jets splashing down onto my belly.

———

"HOW MUCH TROUBLE ARE YOU IN?"

Nearly an hour had passed since Roman pulled me up off the floor and led me to the stairs.

We took a shower together, each of us taking turns to wash the other. Now we lay in his bed. We hadn't talked much and his question sort of caught me off guard.

I hitched up a shoulder and focused my attention on the window. Evening had come and gone, and night had settled around us, bringing with it a heavy, steady downpour. Rain beaded on the windows. I stared at the glass so hard, my eyes started to blur.

"What's that mean?" he asked, voice rough with drowsiness. "No trouble? You don't know? A little trouble?"

I lifted my head and peered at him through the darkness. "I think that might be the most words you've ever spoken to me."

"Talking is overrated."

I thought I caught a hint of a smile from him, but I couldn't be sure.

"Are you going to answer my question?"

I sighed and snuggled in closer to him. "I don't know yet," I told him truthfully. "I tried to go in on Monday but was told to go home. I'm on unpaid leave while they work this thing out."

"I'm sorry," he said.

I could tell by his tone that he meant it. Nodding, I resumed my study of the window, watching the rain bead and collect on the glass.

"What's the deal with that Stilwell guy? Is he just a natural-born asshole?"

That startled a laugh out of me. "I'm going to have to assume it's his natural, God-given gift, Roman."

"He has it out for you, doesn't he?"

"Yeah." I blew out a breath and tried to ignore the tension trying to creep back into my body. "He has, almost from day one. Doing petty-ass things, like calling me Alex and making sure to always be somewhere else when I need his help with one thing or another." Making a face, I added, "For some reason that I can't quite figure out, I'm paired to work with him more than anybody else at the park."

"You don't like being called Alex."

I couldn't stop it. I stiffened. Slowly, I sat up, dragging one of the blankets around me as my body chilled. Already missing his warmth, I folded my legs and pondered my answer. Would he think it was petty? Or that I was being overly emotional?

Fear that he would do just that almost locked my throat, and I told myself to just tell him that it didn't matter, that it wasn't a big deal.

But it was.

And instead of brushing it off, I found myself saying, "I'm named after my father."

Roman's fingers brushed across my spine.

"He was my best friend," I said, my voice going tight and rough. "I had other friends, did well in school and all, but Dad was my *best* friend. We understood each other so well, we could finish each other's sentences. He taught me how to camp, how to fish. I got into forestry because of him – he'd been taking me out into the mountains to camp or hike for as long as I can remember." Sighing, I closed my eyes against the familiar prick of tears. He'd been gone for two years, and I still couldn't quite believe it. "He died a couple of years ago. He didn't even live long enough to see me graduate."

I sniffed and shifted around until I could see Roman's face in the dim light. "*He* was Alex. He started calling me Lexi when I was just a baby. It's…I dunno, maybe it's silly, but when people call me Alex, I expect to hear my dad reply."

He reached out and caught my hand.

I twined my fingers with his and let him tug me down until I was stretched out against him once more.

"I'm sorry about your dad," he said, voice soft.

"Thank you."

I came awake in a rush, looking around the unfamiliar room while the sound of birdsong echoed outside the windows.

For a few seconds, I didn't even know where I was.

Hearing a rhythmic thumping coming from outside, I got to my feet, dragging the blanket with me so I could look outside.

There was a set of French doors, and I turned the knob, stepping out into the bright, chilly morning.

The rain had stopped sometime during the night, and I drew in a breath of the cold, fresh air.

Following the sound, I moved through the doors and onto a balcony that ran along the back of the house.

Out in the yard, I could see Roman bent over something.

As if he sensed my attention, he stopped what he was doing and started toward the house.

His eyes came up to meet mine, and I raised a hand, but he looked away before I even had a chance to wave.

That was the first indicator that something was wrong.

The second happened just a few seconds after he passed out of my view – a door slammed shut somewhere beneath me.

Still, I didn't let it get to me.

Maybe he just wasn't a morning person.

And I still hadn't apologized to him.

I needed to do that, first and foremost, before we even talked about what had happened between us.

My knees went a little weak at the memory of last night, but I immediately shoved the thoughts aside.

I had things to do.

I didn't know where my clothes were – downstairs in a tangle was my best guess.

I spied a black-and-red-checked flannel shirt and moved to grab it. I slipped it on, then went to make the bed.

I could hear the clanging coming from downstairs before I was even halfway down the steps. I was starting to think this was more than him just not being a morning person, but I didn't let the thought take root. Everything was fine.

Sure, he sounded like a pissed-off bear thrashing around in the back of the house.

But there had to be something else going on.

There was no real reason for him to be mad.

That was what I told myself, and what I kept telling myself, right up until I came to a stop in the kitchen doorway and he caught sight of me.

The look he gave me was lethal, so lethal, I wouldn't have been surprised to look down and find myself bleeding.

"Hi," I said guardedly.

He just grunted and turned back to what he was doing. I flinched at the sound of a heavy iron skillet all but slamming down on the stovetop.

"I've got shit to do," he said in a short tone, his back to me. "I'll make you some breakfast, but then you've got to head out."

I swallowed the knot that had suddenly formed.

"I..." The rest of the words trapped in my suddenly tight throat, and I looked away, staring at the clock hanging on the far side of the kitchen.

"Bacon and eggs are about all I've got," he said, voice still edged and sharp.

I tried to imagine having the conversation with him that I needed to have, when he was in this toxic mood.

No. No way in hell.

A cabinet slammed open, and I drew my shoulders back, staring a hole through him as he grabbed something from inside, then slammed the door with equal force. Something hit the counter. I saw that it was a glass cannister − coffee, most likely. It was a wonder it hadn't broken.

Taking a slow, calm breath, I told myself I should at least get the apology out of the way.

"Roman..."

He cocked his head, and I waited for him to turn at look at me. He never did.

"Can you look at me for a minute? I need to talk to you."

He flicked me a disinterested look over his shoulder, then went back to focusing on what he was doing. "I can hear you well enough without looking at you, Lexi. What do you want?"

The admonishment hit me like a slap, and I drew back, the pain I'd been feeling slowly morphing into anger.

"You know what?" I said, pasting a frozen smile on my face. "Fuck it. And I'm not in the mood for breakfast."

I turned on my heel and strode away.

MY HEAD WAS POUNDING.

I hadn't lied when I told Roman I wasn't in the mood to eat.

But one thing I couldn't skip was coffee. Sure, it wasn't the healthiest lifestyle choice, guzzling coffee in lieu of actual fuel, but it worked for me.

I'd been awake for less than thirty minutes when I pulled my Jeep out of the gravel driveway, leaving Roman behind me.

He hadn't even said anything when I stalked through the kitchen and out onto the back porch. I hadn't been able to find my keys or my phone and hoped they were there, so I wouldn't have to keep poking around under the weight of his angry glare.

They were there, my phone in its pseudo-leather wallet case and the keys resting on top of it. Yesterday, I had been so worried about Roman, I had totally forgotten about the keys and phone.

Grabbing them, I strode around the house, taking the path I'd used yesterday as I searched for Roman. Part of me wondered if I shouldn't have just climbed back into my Jeep after he hadn't answered the door, but I'd worried that if he'd kept on sleeping, it was entirely possible he'd never wake up. Hypothermia would have killed him.

It was possible that the dumb bastard was alive because of me.

And there he was, acting like a bear with a thorn in his paw.

"Screw him," I told myself as I unlocked my vehicle and swung inside. My left ankle twinged a bit from the force of the movement, but the brace held firm. Once inside the Jeep, I took one last look at the house, then I started the car.

I needed caffeine before I could even figure out what to do next.

"HEY!"

The bright chipper voice coming from my left had dread curling inside of me.

I grabbed a plastic lid for the coffee I'd just made and turned. Cass Sayer stood there, a surprised smile on her face. "Running into each other again," she said.

"Looks like." I made a show of checking my watch, then looked back at her. "I've got to get moving though."

"Of course."

The line was dragging on insanely slow, and there were still four people ahead of me when Cass fell in behind me.

"Did you find the house okay?" she asked softly.

I half-turned to look at her. With a nod, I said, "No problem." Because I didn't want her to linger on this discussion, I asked, "How is your arm doing?"

"Healing up, I assume." She shrugged and glanced at my casted wrist. "I know you got hurt that night. What happened?"

I gave the wrist a look of disgust. "There was a trapper's snare in the path and…" I sighed, shaking my head. "Anyway, it's fractured."

"Can you do your job okay with a casted wrist?" she asked hesitantly.

I shouldn't have said anything. But I was tired, stressed, and now I had to deal with playing nice instead of just leaving as I wanted to. "For the time being, I won't be doing my *job* at all. I'm on unpaid leave."

Her eyes widened. "What?"

Already wishing I hadn't opened my mouth, I shook my head and looked away. "It's not your problem."

"If it has anything to do with the night my plane went down, I'd have to argue," she said, a line appearing between her brows. She hesitated a second, then asked, "Is it because Roman pretty much conned you into helping him?"

The line in front of me finally moved, and I shuffled forward a whopping foot and a half. "It doesn't matter," I said, trying to keep the edge out of my voice.

"So, that's a yes," she said, sounding annoyed. "First you get hurt out trying to help me, and now my boneheaded brother-in-law has caused your problems."

"I caused my problems," I told her, shaking my head. "I'm the one who made the boneheaded decision to go out with the bonehead."

"And what else were you going to do? If you left him alone, he would have just gone on his own."

I sighed. "Look, can we just drop it?"

I finally made it through the line and was almost to the door when Cass caught up with me.

"Did you tell Roman?" she asked, shoving the door open for me and letting me pass first.

"Tell him what?"

"That your job is in jeopardy because he's a dumbass."

I couldn't help it. I smiled a little. But I shook my head. "It's my concern, not his."

"If you weren't going out to yell at him, what did you go out there for?" she asked reasonably. There was a shrewd look in her eyes, and I had no doubt that she had definitely noticed that I was wearing the same clothes I'd been wearing when we ran into each other the previous day.

I opened my mouth, then closed it, trying to figure out the best way to respond to that. I decided, in the end, to tell her the truth or at least enough to satisfy her so she'd let this all go.

"I wanted to ask him for his help," I told her. Somebody came down the sidewalk, and I stepped aside to let him pass, never once looking away from Cass's face.

"For what?"

"It doesn't matter. He seems to be pretty pissed off today, so I'll just have to handle it on my own."

I could tell she wanted to ask more, but I wasn't in the mood for it, so I shook my head. "I need to get going. I've got a lot to get done today."

I headed for my car, not looking back at her even once.

TWENTY
ROMAN

"So. Let me guess...you were a total asshole when Lexi came out here."

Normally, a visit from Cass was a welcome intrusion. She was one of the few connections I had left of a life when I'd been happy.

But Cass was...well. She didn't pull punches, and when she was pissed, she let everybody in the whole world know it.

Without even looking at her, I knew that her ire was directed at me.

Again.

I seemed to excel at pissing people off these days.

I glanced at her as I adjusted my grip on the heavy branch that had been knocked down during one of the winter storms. I probably wasn't anybody's version of old – at least, anybody over the age of twenty – but the life I'd lived had taken its toll on my body and the last thing I'd wanted to do in the cold and wet that followed one of the storms out here was come out and deal with fallen branches and limbs.

The land I'd inherited from my family had been in our possession for a long time, and any given season brought with it its own share of work. Winter had finally passed, and that meant dealing with the debris from the storms, repairing any of the fences that needed repairing and general clean-up. Not to mention the small garden I was still trying to care for – it had once been my mother's pride and joy, and Ryan had mentioned that he'd like to get it going again.

I couldn't care less about the garden, but I cared about my brother, and my parents.

He'd wanted to start a garden like Mom's, so I'd damn well make sure there was a garden like Mom's.

I passed on the extra vegetables and fruit to Cass and her aging parents, which made me feel like I was doing *something* to help them out. Not much, but something.

"Nice to see you, too, Cass," I said wryly. "It sounds like you're recovering from your ordeal, might I add."

"Oh, kiss my ass," she retorted sharply. "And damn it, drop that branch and look at me when I'm talking to you."

The rebuke was an echo of what Lexi had said to me not even an hour earlier. I dropped the branch and turned to face my sister-in-law. We were closer than that, really. The three of us, Cass, Ryan and me, we'd grown up together. Cass had known for years that Ryan was the one for her, and the bond the two of us shared was more brother and sister than anything else. I loved her dearly. Although I sometimes questioned my intelligence these days, there was one thing that I was still smart enough to understand – Cass in a temper wasn't somebody to mess around with.

Unless, of course, I was looking for a fight.

I didn't often pick fights with my sister-in-law, but some days, I just wasn't in the right frame of mind to avoid them.

With exaggerated care, I dropped the heavy limb and turned to face her. Stripping off my gloves, I tossed them to the ground and met her gaze. "So. What's the problem, honey?"

"Don't call me *honey*, you big ass," Cass snapped, closing the distance between us.

She reached up and jabbed her fingernail into my chest.

The sight of that pink tip skewering me made me scowl. She hadn't painted her nails – that I knew of – since right before Ryan's funeral. Cass was athletic and loved the outdoors, but at the same time, she was innately...well, she'd hate the word *girly*, but that's what she was. Or what she had been. She never left the house without some light touch of makeup, and once a week, she'd gone to get manicures and pedicures. Ryan used to tease her about it.

Hoping to distract her from whatever had set her off, I said, "Nice nails."

"Nice try," she replied with a smirk. "I'm not getting distracted...*honey*. So, tell me. When Lexi was out here, did you just fuck her then kick her out of your bed, or what?"

The blunt, curt comment stung.

The *truth* of it stung even more. Setting my jaw, I caught her wrist and nudged her hand away.

"I don't know what you're talking about." When had she seen Lexi, anyway? How did she know Lexi had been out here?

She shook her head, giving me a look like I was just the dimmest bulb in the pack. "I ran into her yesterday morning – and today. She was wearing the same clothes, both times. Either she's got a limited wardrobe, or she had some unplanned sleepover." She batted her lashes at me. "If it wasn't with you, I'm going to have to find out who it was... you know how much I enjoy gossip."

I resisted the urge to snarl at her. "Fine. She was here. What of it?"

"I'm just wondering why she looked like some puppy you'd kicked when I ran into her," Lexi said with an arch look.

"I don't know what you're talking about." I heard the lie as clearly as she did, and she knew it.

She shook her head and sighed, averting her gaze. "Want to know something?" she asked softly.

Not really, but I wasn't going to tell her that. Instead, I just waited.

"You haven't shown any real sign of life for the past few years, Roman. Ever since Ryan died."

I flinched at the sound of his name. I went to turn away, and she caught my arm.

"I loved him too," she said, her voice thick.

"I know you did."

"And I also know that if he knew how we'd both gone and shut ourselves down after he died, he'd come after us and haunt us until we straightened up." She tipped her head back, staring up at me. Tears glittered in her eyes.

As one broke free to roll down her cheek, I reached up, wiping it away.

I couldn't tell her that I was already haunted. She'd want to know why.

She surprised me then by lifting both hands and cupping my face, forcing me to keep looking at her.

"It wasn't your fault," she said gently. "I know you blame yourself. But it wasn't your fault. You both made a choice, a choice to do a very dangerous job that only a few people can do. You both knew that each mission could be your last." Her voice broke, and she let go of me, using her fingertips to swipe the tears from her cheeks. "You both knew. And sadly, for Ryan, that *was* his last mission. But he died doing something you both believed in, Roman. Protecting this country. And it's pretty shitty of you to take from his sacrifice by insisting that *you* are the only reason he's gone. Because you're not."

She turned away just as I flinched, the impact of her words like salt in an open wound.

And she just kept piling it on too. With her back to me, she asked, "You've got a thing for her, don't you?"

I didn't have to ask who. But I wasn't going to confirm her suspicions, either.

She turned back to me, giving me a cool look.

I jerked my gaze away from hers. "What does it matter?"

"It matters because this is the first time you've actually let yourself feel something since he died. And you're shutting her out, you're shutting those feelings out." She reached out and caught my hand. "If it had been the other way around, if it had been you instead of Ryan, and he came home a shadow of himself, blocking everybody, including me, out…would you be happy about that?"

It was such a simple question.

And the answer to it was equally simple. Yet, I didn't want to voice it.

With Cass, I didn't have to. She saw the answer in my eyes, and she laid her hand on my cheek. "Even if you insist on blaming yourself, surely you've paid the price. Don't you think?"

She turned then and left.

I managed to stay upright long enough for the sound of her truck to fade.

But then I went to my knees and covered my face with my hands.

Back when we'd been kids, the two of us would have razzed the other endlessly for crying.

I couldn't stop the flood, though.

It had been waiting for a long, long time.

MY KNEE GROANED as I pushed myself harder and faster, driving myself up the steep incline of the mountain road with relentless focus.

It had been nearly three hours since Cass left, and I'd spent most of it in a numb haze.

But then thoughts of Lexi crept into my mind, echoed by Cass's comment that Lexi had looked like an abused puppy. It wasn't exactly the comparison I would have made when it came to Lexi. But the thought of her looking hurt, scared, and confused pissed me off, and it was even worse since I knew I was the reason behind it.

My inner logic was already nagging at me, telling me to go and see her, but I didn't have that right.

Not only had I caused problems for her on her job, but she'd been hurt because of me. Then when she came out here and took care of me, then gave herself to me, what had I done?

I'd treated her like shit.

I was ashamed of myself, and I knew if Ryan was here, he'd be ashamed too.

Guilt was an ever-present companion for me, so it wasn't anything new to deal with, but this time, it felt…different.

Grief didn't entitle me to be an ass.

Grief didn't entitle me to make decisions that endangered others.

Grief didn't entitle me to cause problems for others.

And yet, I'd allowed the guilt that had haunted me since Ryan's death to dictate my actions. Almost every day.

This time, there had been consequences, serious ones.

But I wasn't the one suffering those consequences. It was Lexi.

I'd fucked her life up good and proper and when she came out here to see me, I'd just been an asshole.

It's what you're best at, a snide voice inside me muttered.

I silenced it and focused on my breathing, on the pull and flex of muscles as I pounded up the mountain.

I pushed myself harder, faster.

But even after pushing myself to the limit and then some, the guilt was still there, along with a quiet voice, one that was the echo of Cass's…

It wasn't your fault.

BY SEVEN O'CLOCK THAT EVENING, I was so exhausted, it took all my strength to drag my sorry ass into the shower to scrub away the sweat and dirt of the day.

My energy had all but faded away by the time I was able to climb into bed. No sooner did my head hit the pillow was I asleep.

At least, I thought I was asleep.

A low, sardonic voice echoed out of the darkness around me.

"She always was able to kick our asses when we needed it, wasn't she?"

That familiar voice had me jerking upright.

I was in bed. Or I thought I was.

But there was no way I could be hearing that voice.

Ryan's voice.

Scrubbing at my eyelids, I shook my head to clear it, then peered into the dark again.

I was in my room.

Maybe I was imagining…

"You're not imagining things, dumb ass."

Ryan was in front of me.

I sucked in a breath at the sight of him.

The last time I'd seen him, he'd been in full combat gear, helmet, night vision goggles, camo, and armor.

Now he wore an AC/DC shirt and a faded pair of jeans. The shirt was mine.

He always stole it from me.

I hadn't seen it in years, not since I tucked it away inside the empty coffin that had been buried and placed in a grave in lieu of his body.

Tears burned my eyes, and I looked at him through a veil of them. "Ryan?"

"Who else would it be? Santa Claus?" He came over and dropped down on the bed next to me.

"I'm dreaming, aren't I?"

"Yeah."

"So, it's not really you...this is my subconscious, or whatever."

Ryan snorted. "Sure, you go ahead and believe that. But you and I both know that you're the martyr through and through. If this was just your subconscious, you'd be dreaming about us that last night, when the mission went to shit. When have you ever dreamed about me showing up to just tell you that you're being a dumb-ass?"

He had a point.

But he was dead, and the only explanation was that I was dreaming.

I studied him, and he grinned back at me, that familiar, crooked grin.

"You like her, don't you?"

I didn't have to ask who he was talking about.

Looking away, I stared out the window. Outside, instead of the night dark landscape I expected to see, there was just...gray. A silvery, endless expanse of it.

"What does it matter?" I asked softly.

"It matters because you *like* her," he said, that sardonic edge back in his voice. "You haven't paid attention to a woman since that last leave we took over in Paris. What was her name again?"

He knew as well as I did. She'd been coming on to him, but he only ever had eyes for Cass and he'd nudged her in my direction. It wasn't so much *her* that caught my attention, though. And he knew it.

It was the fact that she was warm and soft and clean, everything we'd missed out on when we were in action.

"Cosette," I murmured, trying to summon up an image of her to mind. But the best I managed was black hair, and the longer I tried to pull up a memory of her, the worse it got.

"You can't really remember what she looks like because she didn't much matter beyond the physical," Ryan said. "That's not the case with Lexi. I bet you anything that if you think of *her* right now, you can recall everything down to the finest detail – hell, you probably have a good idea what size bra she wears."

I scowled at him and shoved up off the bed.

I took one step and then turned back to him.

"What does it matter if I can recall *details*?" I said sourly. "I caused her enough trouble. Hell, she could have broken her neck being out there on a night like that. She might lose her job. I bet she can recall plenty of details about me, too – starting and ending with the fact that I fucked up her life."

"You made a mistake," Ryan said easily. He shrugged it off like it didn't matter. "And please remember, you're not the hero of the universe. She made the choice to go with you. She could have just left your sorry ass to do it on your own."

"It would have been better if she had."

"For who?" Ryan asked, sounding genuinely curious. "You? Her?"

"Her," I replied. "I've caused her enough trouble."

"So you've said." He shoved up off the bed and paced

over until just a few inches separated us. "Maybe you should stop thinking about all the problems you caused. They're in the past, and let me tell you, nobody can tell you how stupid it is to dwell on the past when there's no future left for them to dwell on."

I closed my eyes.

"Hey, hey…" Ryan caught my arms and shook me lightly. "It's okay. I made my choice. If it had been you…" He stopped and looked away. "I wish it hadn't been either of us, but I'd rather me be the only one to go down than for it to have happened to you or anybody else on the team. I had one hell of a life. Now it's your turn, brother. Go after that sexy girl, man. Go after her, and if she *lets* you catch her…you better hold on tight."

I WOKE UP ABRUPTLY.

The echo of Ryan's voice still sounded in my ears as I sat up on the edge of the bed.

Go after her.

I waited for the knee-jerk reaction that would inevitably follow, the one that told me I didn't deserve to go after her, that I didn't deserve to be happy.

But for once, it was silent.

I scrubbed my hands over my face as the dream slowly fell to pieces around me, like threads of cotton candy caught in a summer downpour.

Go after her.

I shoved myself upright and I made, a decision.

I was going to do just that.

THIS WHOLE BUSINESS SUCKED.

That was my current frame of mind, and I didn't expect it to change any time soon, either.

I'd been out retracing my steps for the past hour and a half. Although it wasn't snowing, the day had gotten warmer and with that came another set of perils.

Mud.

It sucked at my feet with almost every step, and if it wasn't for the hiking pole I'd elected to take, I suspected I would have gone down more than once.

Even with my tightly laced boots and ankle brace, I didn't entirely trust my ankle, so I had to move at a far slower pace than normal. The last thing I wanted was to fall and possibly re-break my wrist.

By the time I reached the fallen tree where I'd gotten hurt, I was sweating and tired and pissed. I searched around the fallen maple that had obscured the snare and couldn't find it.

I wasn't surprised, of course.

Somebody had removed it.

Frustrated beyond all belief, I tugged off my hat and shoved my hand through my hair. It was damp from sweat. The weather was finally showing some signs of spring. It was still fairly cool, but I'd been at this long enough to work up a sweat.

I was ready for a break. For a moment, I pondered the ranger station we'd used that night.

Memories of Roman tried to creep up on me, but I pushed them away.

The last thing I needed to do was dwell about the night I'd spent with him.

Nights. Plural. I'd spent two amazing, wonderful nights with him. And he hadn't been a complete tool, either. At least not when we'd been pressed up close together.

But as soon as there was distance between us, he'd gone and turned into an asshat.

"Stop thinking about him," I muttered to myself. "Think about *anything* else."

My ankle ached, and I focused on that, and the itchy, sweaty skin under the cast on my wrist. My belly grumbled, and although I'd been drinking water steadily, I felt parched from thirst.

All in all, I was in a lousy mood, and it didn't help that I hadn't been able to find a single trap or snare.

Somehow, the poachers had known to move the one that had injured me, and I was having a hard time believing there had been *just* that one.

I neared a fork in the trail and slowed down out of

habit. It was as I pulled out the map that something occurred to me.

Something that bothered the hell out of me.

My pulse hitched a beat, and my blood started to pound hot and hard.

I couldn't write off the possibility that maybe the poacher, whoever he was, just moved his traps around from time to time, but there was another option.

Somebody had told the poacher it needed to be moved, and fast. They would have *had* to be quick about it, because I knew Hawthorne had been out looking for it early the next morning. Had somebody been desperate enough to go out and remove it that night?

Or maybe it was somebody who'd already been in the area.

I thought of all the rescuers and rangers who'd been tramping through this part of the park that night.

I didn't know how many had gone out for the search and rescue. I could always ask Hawthorne, but until he had come to some sort of decision about my job status, I wasn't about to bother him.

I gave a fleeting thought to talking to the IC from that night. I didn't really know her, but SAR groups tended to rotate through the area, and if she was experienced enough to be the IC, then other search and rescue personnel would likely know her. And she'd know them.

Brooding, I pulled my water from my pack and took a healthy swallow, eyes roaming across the terrain in front of me.

If I didn't find any sign of the poachers today, I'd reach out to Hailey. I hated to think that somebody involved with the SAR groups – or worse, a *ranger* – was involved in this, but in a way, it made sense.

AFTER ANOTHER FORTY-FIVE MINUTES, I made myself stop. My belly was grumbling almost constantly now, and the pain in my ankle had grown rather persistent.

I needed a break.

I settled on an old, dead tree stump and pulled out an energy bar. As I ate, I got my GPS. After I finished the snack, I dug into my pack for the weatherproof map of the park. Spreading it out on my legs, I studied it.

If a poacher had been in the park that night, it was entirely likely they had a base camp set up somewhere in the area.

The trick would be finding it.

Briefly, I thought of a guy I knew. He worked with the state parks and had a canine partner. The dog had helped locate several poachers over the past few years.

Maybe I could enlist him to help on his off-time if I didn't have any luck with Hailey.

A trained canine could definitely expedite matters. Trained to scent the most commonly hunted animals, the dogs were exceptional when it came to locating those animals, which often led to locating people too.

I tucked the idea away and tried to focus on possible locations for the camp.

I tapped one area with my index finger. Whoever was doing this, if they did have a camp, they were either exceptionally lucky or exceptionally knowledgeable of the area.

Although the park was massive, it was routinely patrolled, and areas of concern, when it came to poaching, received even more attention.

But it was possible to elude capture if one knew what he was doing. Much of the park was so isolated, it didn't *get* patrolled, simply because there was just so much land to cover. If the poacher knew which areas to avoid, it would be…well, not simple, but easier to set up a base camp.

Finding somewhere that wasn't likely to catch a ranger's attention would be key. That meant that whoever was behind this, if they did have a camp, was familiar enough with the area and with rangers to know how to avoid suspicion.

Again, I briefly considered whether somebody affiliated with the park, either through SAR teams or through employment, could be behind this.

"Maybe they're working together," I muttered. Scratching at my neck, I pondered that idea and decided it was worth considering. The illegal poaching industry reached into the millions. Places like Mexico provided so-called *canned hunts* and actively courted US travelers to participate in hunts where the animals were caged into one specific area, leaving little room for escape. That wasn't the case here – a canned hunt would catch too much attention and bring down federal officials on any idiot stupid enough to try.

But there were always those willing to break the law for profit. It stood to reason that some skilled trappers were involved in this mess, and if they were somehow working with an official park ranger, they'd be that much more efficient at avoiding capture.

Groaning, I pressed the heel of my hand to my head. A headache pulsed beneath my palm.

I was tired and sore and hungry. The energy bar hadn't done much more than fill the hole in my belly, and I wasn't in the mood for any of the food I'd stuffed into my daypack, either.

But I wasn't quite ready to give up my search just yet.

Focusing on the map, I studied the marks around the area that had caught my attention. It wasn't near any trails. There was a healthy spring that ran through the middle of that area, and any decent outdoorsmen would know that where there was water, they'd find animals.

I punched the coordinates into my GPS and pondered the route I'd have to take.

It would be a rough one, but as long as I was careful, I could make it there and back with plenty of time before sundown. But if I was going to do that, I needed to eat something more than an energy bar. I also needed to tend to personal matters, and while I was equipped to do it sans facilities, there was an outhouse not far away. I just had to trek back to the ranger station we'd used last week.

TWENTY-TWO
ROMAN

"I...I'm sorry, Roman, but could you please repeat that?"

I squeezed my eyes shut. The humor in Cass's voice was clear, but since she'd given me a much-needed kick in the pants, I figured I could take her prodding. "I said you were right."

"I thought I'd *never* hear those words from you," she said, laughter coloring her words.

"Ha, ha. You're right more often than I am, and you know it."

"True...but you rarely acknowledge it."

I snorted. "Okay. Now that you've had your fun, I wanted to let you know I'm going to talk to Lexi."

She was quiet for so long, I almost wondered if the call had dropped. But then she cleared her throat and said, "Wow. That's surprising. Did I kick you in the ass or what?"

"It wasn't just you," I said, my mind drifting back to my dream about Ryan.

"Then what was it?" she asked softly.

I hesitated, reluctant to go into detail. But if anybody would understand, it was Cass. "I had a dream about Ryan."

She didn't speak, so I continued. "It was…it was weird. Not dreaming about him, because I do that all the time. But we're always back overseas, on that last mission. This time, it was like he was right here with me. He was wearing my AC/DC shirt."

"The one he kept swiping from you," she said, her voice husky. "It drove you nuts when he did that." She sniffed before continuing, "You put it in the coffin."

"Yeah." Now it was my turn to clear my throat. "He knew it drove me crazy when he took it. That's why he did it."

I was surprised that I could think about it. Cass joined in, but the sound faded after just a few seconds.

"Anyway, he basically told me what you've been telling me for months."

"That you need to quit being a dipshit and stop blaming yourself?" she suggested. The words came out thick, like she might be trying not to cry.

"Cass…"

"It's okay. *I'm* okay," she insisted. "Go on. Finish telling me."

"There's not a whole lot to tell. He told me to get my head out of my ass, then he asked if I might have a thing for Lexi."

"Which, of course, you do."

I smiled a little at her arched tone. "Yeah. I think I've got a thing for her."

"So are you going to go after her?" she asked.

"Yeah. I'm actually getting ready to head up to Estes Park now. A friend of mine got her address for me."

"Maybe she's back at work."

I wanted to think that was possible, but I wasn't about to set up any such expectations. "If she is, I'll just track her down."

I was about to end the call when Cass asked, "Did she ever tell you what she needed your help with?"

"My help?" I frowned, thinking back to her visit.

"I guess not," Cass said wryly. "When I ran into her at the gas station that first day, she said she was looking for you because she needed your help with something."

"No," I told her, disgusted with myself. "She never mentioned anything."

She was too busy dragging my sorry ass out of the cold, then I was too busy dragging her excellent ass under me. I pinched the bridge of my nose as I said, "I'll figure out what it was."

"Good." She paused a moment, then added, "It's good to see you trying to come back into the land of the living, Roman. I've missed you."

She ended the call before I could respond.

Once more, guilt tried to well up inside me, but I shoved it down.

I'd spent enough time wallowing in self-pity and self-loathing.

Right now, I needed to talk to Lexi.

SHE WASN'T AT HOME. There was no vehicle in the driveway, but I knocked just to be sure.

After giving it a minute, I knocked again.

The house had that quiet feel of an empty home – no music playing, no lights on, no TV.

I knocked twice more, then left.

Maybe Cass was right. Maybe she was back at work. A part of me hoped that was the case. It would mean I hadn't totally ruined things with her job.

As I drove toward the park entrance, I tried to figure out the right words to use when I saw her.

She was likely to be pissed off at me, and I couldn't blame her.

I couldn't even blame her if she didn't want to speak to me again, but I was hoping I could convince her to forgive me.

And I wanted to know what she'd needed my help with. Once I made things right between us again, I'd find out and then we'd deal with whatever it was together.

I got to the visitor's center inside the park and parked the truck. On my way inside, I looked at the small crowd of people forming, eyes narrowing in on a slim female form clad in the familiar tan and green uniform of the rangers. Almost immediately, I knew it wasn't Lexi. Disappointed, I continued on up to the visitor's center, keeping an eye out for her.

A few minutes later, the disappointment got even worse.

The lady behind the counter gave me a polite smile and told me that Lexi was taking a few days off. I didn't bother asking anymore and turned to head back outside.

A familiar form was striding my way, his eyes on the phone he held.

I moved to intercept him, making an attempt at a polite smile.

Judging by the way he was looking at me, I either failed, or he was still pissed at me for putting him on the spot in front of his boss.

"Stilwell." I rocked back on my heels as I met his gaze.

He just stared at me.

"I'm trying to find Lexi. Have you seen her?"

This elicited a smile from him, and he reached up to scratch at his chin. "Out for a booty call there, Sayers? I haven't seen Alex. You'd have better luck–"

I shot out a hand and grabbed him by the front of his perfectly ironed shirt. Jerking him close, I snarled, "Watch how you talk about her, you piece of shit. And for the record, her name is *Lexi*. You keep on trashing or using the wrong name, I'm going to rip your tongue out and tie it into a knot…while you watch."

He eyed me narrowly, his hands prying at my fist, but I didn't let go until I was good and ready.

When I did, I gave him a hard shove that sent him stumbling back more than a few feet.

"Now…let me ask that question again. Have you seen Lexi?"

He sneered at me. "Why should I tell you a fucking thing?"

"For starters…" I took a menacing step toward him. "I would very much *enjoy* ripping your tongue out and tying it into a knot. For another, if you don't, I'm going to hunt down your boss and ask him what the deal is with Lexi not being at work…since *you* are the one who told her to take me out."

His lids flickered, although the sneer remained in place. "She made her own choices, you know. I didn't force her to do anything. But, for the record, I haven't seen her." He smoothed his wrinkled shirt as he continued, "The official reason is that she's taking some more time off to heal, but everybody knows it's because she acted unprofessionally. And on top of breaking protocol, she tried to lie her way out of it, claiming there was an illegal snare in the woods that caused her injury."

Illegal.

I eyed him speculatively. He went to go around me, but I stepped into his path.

"Something you might want to consider, Stilwell." I gave him a cold smile. "Lexi wasn't out there alone. I'm surprised your boss hasn't reached out to me to ask my side of the story. Maybe I should just go track him down while I'm here."

He didn't even blink.

But there was…something. A faint tightening around his eyes, the way his mouth flattened out just the slightest. Something.

Silence stretched out and dragged on until he abruptly cleared his throat. "You aren't going to have much luck finding him. He's got a meeting elsewhere, then he's going to be out in the park for the next few days, checking out trails and stations to make sure they don't need to be cleared of any debris from the winter snow."

"Aw, that's alright. I'm patient. I can wait."

He said nothing else, just cut sharply around me and stomped into the visitor's center.

Turning my attention to the trees, I debated, then headed back to my truck.

I was acting on instinct now, but under most circumstances, my instincts had typically done an alright job in steering my decisions. It was about time I started trusting them again.

I FOUND Lexi's Jeep parked near the entrance to the unmarked trail we'd taken that night.

If she hadn't come out to my place, I wouldn't have been able to pick her vehicle out. Eying the silvery-gray Jeep, I parked behind her and got out of the truck and moved to circle the vehicle.

The hood was cool, so the engine had been off for a little while.

Without giving it another second, I turned back to my car and retrieved the pack I'd used that night. I'd already replaced the few supplies I'd used, and before I'd left the house, I had taken a few minutes to refill the water bladder concealed inside the pack.

It was easier to navigate the trail this time around. It was still daylight and warmer, no snow coming down to obscure my vision. The path was muddy though, an annoyance I could have done without. But I'd been out in worse conditions, so I ignored it and trucked on.

As I walked, I saw signs that somebody else had been on the path before me sometime recently. I could make out the smaller footprints, the tread resembling that of the boots I wore. She took smaller steps than I did, but it took more than an hour before I came across any sign of her other than the tracks.

I reached the fallen piece of timber that had barred the path when Lexi had gotten hurt. It had been moved from the middle of the trail, but I knew this was the right place. She'd been here for a few minutes, at least, judging by the path her boots had left.

A look farther down the path showed that it hadn't been used in the past few hours, so I studied the tracks again, spying where she'd turned around and started to backtrack.

It wasn't hard to figure out where she was going and as I followed her trail, I started to move faster.

I didn't know why she was out here, but I had an idea, and if I was right, she could be walking straight into a hornet's nest.

By the time I reached the smaller path that led to the ranger station, I was moving at a slow jog. I could see the timbers of the building up ahead, and I forced myself to slow down.

Caution dictated that I take a few minutes to assess the situation, but it was warring with my need to make sure Lexi was okay.

As I broke through the clearing, she came walking around the building. At the sight of her, my chest expanded and an ache I hadn't even been aware of started to fade.

She was wearing hiking shorts, a sweatshirt, and a cap,

along with thick-soled hiking boots on her feet. She didn't have a pack, but a quick look around assured me she'd just left it behind for a few minutes. I spotted the familiar back-pack sitting by the porch, along with her canteen.

I took a step in her direction. "Lexi."

TWENTY-THREE

LEXI

I yelped at the sudden appearance of Roman. The sound of my name in the quiet woods was startling enough that I jumped, and a twinge in my left ankle had me swinging up my hand to steady myself against the outside wall of the nearby ranger station.

My *left* hand.

Sharp pain shot up my arm and I glared at him. Bringing my arm in close to my chest, I demanded, "What in the hell are you doing, sneaking up on me like that?"

And *why* hadn't I heard him? Sound traveled pretty damn far when you were in such a vast space with no people. Or *almost* no people.

"What in the hell are *you* doing?" he fired back at me. "There are poachers running around, and you've got a bad ankle *and* a broken wrist."

"My ankle is *fine*, thank you," I said with a sniff, choosing to ignore how it had been aching for the past little while.

"Yeah, and that's why you grabbed for the building –

with your *left* hand because your wrist is feeling so good."
He came toward me, and before I realized what he was up
to, he swept me into his arms and carried me over to the
small, square porch. He lowered me down and hunkered in
front of me, reaching for my left foot.

I pulled back as much as I could. "I'm *fine*. Don't you
have a lot of shit to do? Why are you even *here*?"

He reached up to touch my cheek, but he must have
seen the look on my face – the one that said, *touch me and die.*

Sighing, he lowered his hand and studied me. "I was an
ass the other day. I'm sorry."

I averted my eyes and stared out into the trees. Sunlight
peeked through the leaves, shining down here and there,
dust motes dancing in the air. "Fine. You're sorry. You went
to an awful lot of trouble to come out here and tell
me that."

"It's not just that."

He was quiet for so long, I gave into the urge and looked
at him. He seemed to be waiting for just that, because once
our eyes met, he said, "I couldn't stand the thought of you
being out here alone. If something happened to you…"

He didn't continue, just rose and paced away. He
reached for the chest strap on his back and freed it, shrugging out of it with sharp, jerky motions. He dropped it to
the ground and turned away, staring into the trees.

"I mean, I came out to the park to apologize, but you
weren't there, and that fuck Stilwell mentioned that you
were in trouble for what happened – another thing I need
to apologize for – and then he mouthed off about how
you'd made up the thing about the snare. I worried you
might be out here looking for evidence, and I freaked out.

If the poachers know you're onto them, it's not safe out here. Every second it took me to find you was a minute too long."

"It's not your problem," I said, still stinging from his rebuff the other day. My ego had taken too much crap over the past few days, and I was leery about letting my guard down.

"The hell it's not," he said, turning to face me. His expression was hard, eyes practically opaque with rage. "*I'm* the reason you got into this mess. *I'm* the reason you got hurt. *I'm* the reason you're in trouble with your boss. It damn well is my problem."

The intensity of his voice caught me off guard.

He took a step toward me.

Nervous, I curled my fingers around the edge of the porch, the worn old wood, smoothed with age, digging into my palm.

"I've already lost one person because I dragged them along with me."

I frowned at the words, not quite following.

"I'm not losing somebody else. I'm not going to risk something happening to you."

"I…" My throat locked, trapping the words inside me, and I had to clear it twice before I could speak. "What in the world are you talking about?"

"You being out here. It's dangerous. You have to know how ruthless some poachers are."

Shaking my head, I said, "That's not what I'm talking about. You said you lost somebody…"

His gaze fell away. A heavy sigh shuddered out of him, and he dragged his hands up and down his face before looking back at me. "My brother," he said in a hoarse voice. "I lost my brother. My twin. Ryan."

I was still confused. "I...Cass told me he was killed in action. That isn't your fault."

"It damn well is," he replied, voice level, almost remote. "He joined the army, so we wouldn't be separated. I'd made it clear I was signing up, and he wasn't going to let us be split up. If I hadn't joined the army, if I hadn't gone on and become a Ranger, he'd still be alive. He was on that mission because of *me*." He jabbed his thumb at his chest and looked away again. "It's my fault."

My heart started to ache for him.

"What happened?" I asked softly.

"An IED. An improvised explosive device." He looked uncomfortable now. Closing his eyes, he lifted his face to the sky. "We were on a mission. We were closing in our target, and the group he was with...they think he was probably the one to step on it. It killed him and one other guy, injured three more. We took heavy fire trying to evac, and another guy was shot and killed. Three of us gone, just in a blink. And Ryan was one of them."

Rising, I went to him, my heart aching.

"It wasn't your fault," I told him softly.

I laid my hand on his cheek, and he covered it with his own. "But–"

"No," I said, pressing my finger to his lips. "It wasn't your fault. Your brother was a grown man and made his own choices, just like you."

"Lex–" The feel of his mouth moving against my skin, even in such an innocuous manner, made me shiver. Want started to pulse inside me, and I jerked my hand back, curling it into a fist as if that would wipe away the memory of his touch.

But nothing could do that.

My anger at him faded, and I shook my head again. "Don't argue with me, Roman. It *wasn't* your fault." I blew out a breath and looked around. "And it's not your fault – or not *entirely* your fault – that I'm in the mess I'm in. I'm a grown woman, and like you, like your brother, I make my own choices. I knew it was a bad idea to go out with you. I just decided to go against my better judgment."

"Why?" The rough timbre of his voice was like a stroke down my spine. When I didn't respond, he brushed his fingers down my cheek. "Why did you go out with me, Lexi?"

"I was scared you'd get hurt or lost," I said, which was mostly the truth. But I didn't tell him that even in his black, surly mood, I'd felt drawn to him that night. I still did.

"Look at me, Lexi."

I did, slowly, although I knew it wasn't a good idea.

He closed the rest of the distance between us, and there hadn't been much to begin with. "If I'd gotten lost or hurt, it would have been my own damn fault."

"And it's my own damn fault I *did* get hurt," I said pointedly. "Granted, it might have looked better for me if *you* had been the one to get your ankle caught in the snare."

I was surprised to see a grin flash over his face. "I can understand your point." The smile faded quickly, and the intensity returned to his gaze. "You didn't need to feel responsible for me."

"You're big on double standards, aren't you?" Wryly, I

laughed. "You feel this is your responsibility but don't like the fact that I also feel like it's my responsibility."

He had nothing to say to that, his face twisting in a scowl.

I found my gaze lowering to his mouth. I wanted to feel that mouth again.

Like *now*.

And even though I knew it was a huge fucking mistake, I leaned in and pressed my lips to his, giving in to that insane urge.

For a moment, he didn't even move. Sliding my tongue out, I licked the full lower curve of his lip, then pushed inside.

His taste was intense and so, so good. Curling my arm around his neck, I pressed closer.

With a rough groan, he caught me around the hips.

JUST STANDING SO CLOSE TO LEXI AND NOT BEING ABLE TO touch her was an exercise in pure torture, but she'd made it clear she didn't *want* me touching her.

I was about ready to get away, so I wouldn't give in to temptation, but then, in a soft, quiet voice, she said. "It wasn't your fault."

As she spoke, she reached up and laid her hand on my cheek. That light touch blistered through me, soothing old hurts and awakening new ones. Without thinking, I covered her hand with mine.

"But—"

"No." She shook her head and touched her finger to my lips. "It wasn't your fault. Your brother was a grown man and made his own choices, just like you."

"Lex—"

She pulled her hand away and shifted her gaze from mine. "Don't argue with me, Roman. It *wasn't* your fault. And it's not your fault – or not *entirely* your fault – that I'm in the mess I'm in. I'm a grown woman, and like you, like your brother, I make my own choices. I knew it was a bad idea to go out with you. I just decided to go against my better judgment."

"Why?" I studied her face, wanting to read her eyes. But she didn't look at me, and she didn't answer. I tried again, and lightly, hesitantly, I brushed my fingers down her cheek. "Why did you go out with me, Lexi?"

"I was scared you'd get hurt or lost."

I knew that was part of it, but something told me that there was more to it than what she was saying.

"Look at me, Lexi." I moved a little closer, close enough now that my boots almost brushed hers.

Her eyes moved back to mine.

"If I'd gotten lost or hurt, it would have been my own damn fault."

"And it's my own damn fault I *did* get hurt." She rolled her eyes. "Granted, it might have looked better for me if *you* had been the one to get your ankle caught in the snare."

Personally, I wished it had been me. It would have served me right. I smiled a little. "I can understand your point. You didn't need to feel responsible for me."

"You're big on double standards, aren't you?" She laughed. "You feel this is your responsibility but don't like the fact that I also feel like it's my responsibility."

While I was trying to think of a way to respond to that, her gaze dipped to my mouth.

Heat began to pulse inside me, a gut-deep need to touch her again, taste her.

Then she pressed her mouth to mine. I froze, uncertain of how to react. She licked my lips, teasing her way inside. I opened for her, desperate to have her taste on my tongue again. She curled her arm around my neck, and as her breasts crushed against my chest, my control shattered.

Grabbing her, I hauled her in close, gripping her hips. She rocked against me and my cock, already swelling, surged to instant, rampant life.

I caught the back of her neck, pulling her in even tighter until we were pressed together from our mouths to our knees. I wanted to consume her, drown in her, lose myself in her.

Tearing my mouth from hers, I caught her shoulders and eased away, struggling to regain some shred of calm. "If we keep this up, I'm going to have your pants around your ankles in about thirty seconds."

"Promise?" She looked at me with lambent eyes.

"*Fuck*," I muttered, jerking her back up against me.

"Sounds good to me."

I covered that smiling mouth with my own and tugged the band restraining her hair. I dropped it and fisted my hand in the silken, red-gold strands. Sliding my hand up to her waist, I sought out the full curve of her breasts. Naked. I wanted her naked.

A wind picked up, whistling over our heads just as I leaned back, ready to grab her shirt and strip it off.

That was when I stopped to think about where we were. Looking past her shoulder, I nodded at the cabin. "Can we get inside before I get you naked?"

"Yes." She laughed, the sound low and giddy. She pulled me along with her.

I paused just long enough to grab my pack and swung it into place. I hitched up hers before she could do so and waited not so patiently for her to unlock the door. We pushed inside.

I dropped the packs as she turned to me.

Reaching for her, I spun and pulled her with me, backing her up against the door.

"Naked," I said. "I need you naked now."

She went to pull her shirt away, but I beat her to it.

As I dropped it to the floor, she shoved off the flannel I wore, then reached for the hem of my thermal and pushed and pulled until she had it over my head. As I took over the rest of the job, she leaned in and pressed a kiss to my chest.

My shirt fell to the pile on the floor as she reached behind and unfastened her bra.

Her breasts swung free, and I cupped them both in my hands, dipping my head until I could press my face to the valley between her firm, excellent tits. I couldn't even begin to describe how much I wanted her. It was like a cancer, something eating away at me inside, but the only pain it caused was the erotic sort.

She shoved her fingers into my hair and held me close as I shifted my attention to her left nipple, sucking it into my mouth, then using my tongue to circle the swollen, distended tip.

I felt her fingers tugging at my waistband, and I straightened.

"You're over the thirty-second mark, pal," she said with a sly grin. "Just trying to move things along."

"Are you in a hurry?"

"Yes. A hurry to get you naked and inside me."

"Sounds like a plan," I said, reaching for the waistband of her pants and pushing down. Kneeling as I stripped them down, I paused only long enough to untie her boots. "Why are you wearing something so fucking hard to get off? You shouldn't be wearing anything I can't get off in two seconds."

"How about you quit talking and focus on getting *me* off?" She touched her tongue to her lips, her big gray eyes going dark and needy.

"I can do that." I finished yanking off the second boot, then groaned at the sight of the high-rising ankle brace I'd just revealed. "You did this just to torture me."

She laughed.

The bright, happy sound should have been out of place, but I found myself laughing with her. I'd never had this, somebody I could laugh with even in a moment like this.

The laughter faded as I managed to get the brace off, then *finally*, I could strip off her pants. That left her standing in a pair of red panties...and one sock. I decided the sock wasn't an issue and caught the scrap of red, dragging it down her hips, down long, leanly muscled legs.

That done, I caught her hips and leaned closer, nuzzling the curls between her thighs. She gripped my head tightly, a husky moan escaping her lips. The sound of it was pure heaven in my opinion, and the taste of her was every bit as good.

"Roman..."

Her hips rocked in my hands. Closing my mouth around her clit, I drew it into my mouth and swirled my tongue around it.

Her sharp cry shattered the air around us. I did it again, then slid two fingers into her cunt, scissoring them slowly. She whimpered again. Her pussy clamped tight around me, and my dick gave a hard, demanding jerk. The damn thing wanted to be in her – *now* – but I was too busy enjoying the taste of her and feeling her shudder and shake as I ate at her pussy.

I decided we'd compromise, my dick and me. I told him that once I had her coming, he'd get his wish.

And judging by the sounds she was making and the trembling of her body, that wasn't far off.

I was right.

As I went to screw my fingers back inside her cunt again, she broke around me with a strangled cry. I surged to my feet and tore at the button on my jeans. I pushed them down just enough, then picked her up by the hips, boosting her higher.

She wrapped her legs around me as I fit the head of my cock to her entrance.

"Look at me," I ordered.

She did, still shuddering and moaning as the waves of her climax started to fade.

We watched each other as I slid home. The intensity of it was a punch…to my gut, to my heart, to my soul.

I withdrew slowly, the wet heat of her pussy so slippery and sweet and tight. "I'm not wearing a rubber," I said, voice rough.

"I know." She shuddered and wiggled, urging me to move faster, but I didn't want this to be fast or over too soon. "I'm on the pill. Female stuff."

"This is still stupid," I muttered.

"We've already been stupid once." She tugged my face to hers and whispered the rest against my mouth. "Let's be stupid one more time."

I didn't think once would be enough.

But I was done talking. Catching her lower lip between my teeth, I sucked it into my mouth as she curled her arms around my neck.

I felt her nipples stabbing into my chest, rubbing back and forth as I thrust up into her.

So, *so* sweet.

So, *so* perfect.

Her pussy clenched around me, and I groaned. "Don't do that…"

Instead of listening, however, she did it again.

One look at her assured me it was intentional. I froze inside her, almost loathe to move as she milked my cock. It was enough to shove me over the edge, and I began to move in her again, harder, faster.

Her short, neat nails bit into my skin.

Her tongue tangled with mine.

When I broke the kiss, she tugged my face back to hers and caught my lower lip between her teeth, biting down.

The sweet erotic pain was intense. Too intense.

Cupping the back of her head in my hand, I guided her mouth to my neck.

She knew what I wanted – exactly. She bit my neck, sucking on a patch of skin before scoring my flesh with her teeth again.

I swiveled and twisted my hips, and she tore away from me, arching her back with a broken, raw cry.

That sound echoed through me, and I lost it, thrusting harder and faster. Moans and pleas and cries fell from her lips in a litany. I gritted my teeth to keep from making any noise, not wanting to lose one second of hearing her gasp and moan out her pleasure.

Then she started to come.

Her mouth opened in a silent scream and her entire body locked up around me, so tight I had to fight to fuck my way back inside. I did so, enjoying every sweet second of it.

My own orgasm hit hard and fast, knocking the breath right out of me. The rise and rush of sex-induced adrenaline had my head spinning around. As I filled her, she shuddered, draining everything out of me.

Including, it seemed, my strength because as the orgasm stretched on and on and on, my knees went a little weak.

I had to lock them to simply keep standing.

Her cries faded to moans and then to ragged gasps of air as the orgasm finally let her go.

Burying her face against my neck, she whispered, "I love what you do to me, Roman."

I loved what she did to me. Turning my face into her hair, I said, "I'm happy to do it to you any time you want, ma'am."

WE LAY ON THE BED, wrapped around each other.

Not paying attention to the time, we simply enjoyed one another's presence. I had no idea how much time had passed before either of us thought about where we were or the fact that we were still out in the middle of the forest, with the daylight hours waning away.

By the time we did notice, it had gotten incredibly dark within the cabin.

I moved to the window and looked outside. "If we try to hike back in the dark, we're asking for trouble. With the warm weather we've had, the ground is pretty damn wet from the melting snow. Not being able to see well in conditions like these is just asking for trouble."

"I know." She sighed and lifted her splinted wrist, giving it a look of acute dislike. "The last thing I need to do is lose my footing, even a little."

I came up behind her and wrapped my arms around her waist. "We were stupid one more time, like you suggested. What do you say we be smart now...and stay the night here?"

"That's being smart, huh?" She craned her head around and looked at me, a grin on her face. "My luck, Stilwell will find out and go running to Hawthorne."

"Stilwell isn't going to do shit," I promised her. If he caused her *any* more problems, I was going to crush him like the bug he was.

She didn't look convinced but said nothing.

Pulling her in closer, I nuzzled her neck. "He isn't going to keep causing you problems, Lexi. I won't allow it."

"I think you really mean that." She turned in my arms and cuddled up close, one hand closing into a fist, pressing right up against my heart. The simplicity of the gesture caused the piece of meat in my chest to ache in a way it never had before. It was almost like a limb that had gone to sleep and was finally starting to wake.

I kind of liked it.

"What do you say we find what we have to eat in our packs?" she murmured, splaying her fingers wide then curling them back into a fist as if relishing the feel of my skin. "Then we can go to bed."

"I like that plan." I liked it a lot. As a matter of fact, I thought it might just become my favorite plan in the history of all plans. The thought amused me, and I pulled back to kiss her, still smiling.

"What's that grin for?" she asked, peering up at me as I lifted my head.

"Just feeling all-around pleased with the current state of things."

Her nose wrinkled as she eyed me. "We're in a small cabin out in the middle of nowhere with nothing but camp food to eat, and we'll be sleeping on a hard bed that's the equivalent to sleeping on a bag of rocks. And you're pleased."

"The company makes it all worth it," I said softly, cupping her cheek.

A smile bloomed across her face, and she wrapped her arms around me tighter, squeezing me close.

Oh, yeah. This was definitely going to be my favorite plan.

TWENTY-FIVE
LEXI

THE SOUND OF SOMETHING ODD WOKE ME. I SAT UP, PEERING over at Roman before looking around, confused.

I heard the noise again and belatedly realized what it was – and why it seemed so out of place.

A phone was ringing. Sliding from the narrow, lumpy bed, I went over to Roman's pack and found the device tucked into an exterior pocket. The moment I pulled it out, I realized how in the hell he'd managed to pick up a signal way out here.

It was a satellite phone.

Some of the SAR groups I'd worked with had one or two people who carried a sat phone, which was the only reason I recognized what I was looking at.

I saw the name *Cass* on the screen and was debating on answering when I heard Roman heave out a sigh behind me. I turned just in time to see him open sleep-hazed green eyes. I froze, not certain what to do. The last time we were together, he'd been an utter ass. Come to think of it, the first time we'd been together, he'd been pretty distant the next morning too.

I bit my lip and shoved the phone toward him. "Cass is trying to call you."

The phone didn't ring again, and I felt sheepish.

He sat up and held out a hand, but when I went to turn over the phone, he didn't take it. Instead, he caught my wrist and drew me in close, until I stood between his knees. He leaned forward and pressed a kiss to the middle of my torso, then rubbed his stubbled face against my skin. The unfamiliar caress made me shiver.

"Good morning," he murmured.

My heart clenched inside my chest, and I had to clear my throat before I could respond to his greeting.

He continued to hold me, his face tucked against my middle, and I closed my eyes, running my fingers through his shaggy, soft hair with my injured hand. My movement was limited thanks to the cast, and the silk of his hair offered no resistance, so I could caress away and never have a problem.

I still clutched the phone, and when he pulled back to look up at me, I offered it once more.

He took it this time, but instead of using it, he dropped it on the bed next to me.

I gasped as he tumbled me into his lap, shifting me around until I sat across his thighs like an overgrown child. Of course, there was *nothing* childish between us. It was hot, raw and confusing, yes, but not childish.

"How did you sleep?" he asked.

The question caught me off-guard, but I recovered quickly and shrugged. "Better than I expected." I cocked a brow at him. "It might have had something to do with the fact that somebody kept me up until well after midnight."

"I have no regrets." That faint smile curled his lips.

Bending down, I pressed my lips to his. "Me, neither."

We stayed like that for a moment, then I pulled back. We really shouldn't have been here overnight. I had no idea if it was possible for one of the other rangers not to realize I'd been here. All they'd have to do was see my Jeep, and they'd know I was in the park, but I wanted to think that maybe my luck could be good for once.

We needed to get moving.

"Why don't you go ahead and call Cass?"

He let me go, his hands lingering as if he really didn't want to. "Yeah, I should."

I turned away to give him the illusion of privacy, grabbing my pack and rooting through it.

My pack always had enough gear – and clothing – to last me a good two days out in the wilderness, so I had a spare set of clothes. I shot him a quick look, but he'd paced over to the window and was staring down, his back to me. Quickly, I stripped off my shirt and used one of the baby wipes I'd taken to carrying with me. I felt a little bit better once that was done. He was talking in a low voice behind me. Out of courtesy, I tuned the conversation out.

By the time I was done putting on clean if somewhat wrinkled clothes, he was tucking the phone away.

Our gazes met.

"I think Stilwell has my boss convinced there wasn't any snare," I said, surprising myself. I'd resigned myself to the fact that I would have to find proof, and do it alone, but now that Roman was here, I was wavering.

"Stilwell ran his mouth about that when I saw him yesterday – pretty much made it clear he figures you're making it up. I told him otherwise." He flashed me a smile that looked far more relaxed than any I'd ever seen from him. "He didn't seem happy about it."

"That guy is only happy when he's causing *me* trouble."

"You, specifically?" Roman cocked his head, eyes narrowing slightly.

"It seems like." I shrugged restlessly and crouched in front of my pack, searching for something I could eat for breakfast. "He isn't all that great a guy in general. Nobody really seems to like him – I hear the other guys talking about him all the time. But I'm the only one he really goes after and causes problems for."

"Any idea why?"

I pursed my lips as I looked up at him. Deciding to be blunt, I admitted, "I think it's because I have tits."

"Ah." Roman's gaze lowered briefly. Heat washed over me. But his eyes quickly returned to mine. "Personally, those tits don't pose a problem for me."

"If maybe I'd been receptive to his advances, they wouldn't have as much of a problem for him. But not only did I not want to sleep with him, I'm here doing the same job he does. He's made no effort to hide the fact that he's a sexist pig. As far as he's concerned, women belong at home."

"Why haven't you reported him?" Roman asked.

"You got any idea what kind of shit women deal with when they complain about sexual harassment or sexism in the workplace?" I pulled out a couple of granola bars and a bottle of water. "Especially in a field like this. Doing so would just cause me more grief, and it's easy enough for me to ignore him."

I tossed one of the granola bars to Roman. "Here. Nice and full of protein."

He made a face. "Yum."

"They're pretty decent, really. I order them online. Better than a lot of the protein bars out there."

"Sold." He tore into it, and after devouring half of it, he asked, "Mind if I ask what it is you're doing out here?"

"Looking for proof." I sighed and opened the granola bar. I gave the task more focus than it really needed, but even though I thought things between us were level again, I'd never really shared a lot of myself with anybody. Other than my dad. It went against my nature to open myself up. "I love this job, Roman. I've always wanted to do this, and now I'm worried…"

"You think if you turn in proof that there is poaching going on here, it will help you out with your supervisor."

I looked back at him, the granola bar and my hunger temporarily forgotten. "Yes."

He paced over to me and hooked his arms over my shoulders.

"I can always tell your boss that I saw the snare," he offered.

"I don't want you fixing this for me." I shook my head and looked away. He was so close, the scent of him filled my head, and I wanted to lean against him and press my face to his chest, just breathe him in and enjoy the simple warmth of his presence. I didn't allow myself to do that, though. "Even if you were the reason I went against protocol, I still made the mistake. It's up to me to find a way to fix this."

I could sense the intense way he was watching me and suspected that he really wanted to argue. He didn't though.

After a moment, I glanced back at him.

He cupped my cheek in one hand. "Okay. If you feel like you have to fix this, then okay. But I want to help."

My heart slammed against my ribs. "Help, how?"

"I'm going out with you. If we don't find anything today, then we rest, regroup and start looking again tomorrow or the day after. But I want you to wait for me – no taking off without me." A cloud passed through his eyes. "I understand the need to handle things on your own, but you know how dangerous poachers can be. You shouldn't be doing this alone."

"You know," I said slowly. "The main reason I came out to your place the other day was to ask if you'd maybe take a look around here with me." I trailed my fingers along his cheek, letting myself smile. "Then you pulled your Oscar the Grouch routine, and I re-evaluated."

"Hey..." Roman winced. "I apologized for that, didn't I?"

Nodding, I rose onto my toes and pressed my lips to his chin. "I'd love for you to come along with me, Roman. Thank you."

TWENTY-SIX

ROMAN

"WE'RE GETTING CLOSE TO A STREAM," LEXI SAID, PAUSING to glance back at me over her shoulder. "It's probably flooded from the snow melting. I don't know if we've got any chance of finding something there, but if we don't, we can hike north for another hour or two, maybe, then head back."

I calculated the time it would take to do that, then get back to our vehicles and decided we had more than enough time to finish before dark. "Sounds good to me."

As she moved along the trail, muscles flexed in her calves. She carried her pack easily, like she'd been doing this all her life.

"How long have you been doing this?" I asked her.

"Doing what?"

"Hiking. Being out here."

She shot me a grin. "I practically grew up in these woods. My dad gave me my first hiking backpack when I was five – and yes, I carried stuff in it." She wrinkled her nose as she added, "Sure, some of it was stuffed animals, but I was also responsible for carrying my own clothes and my sleeping bag. If I couldn't fit everything I needed into the pack, my animals stayed home."

I laughed, amused and somehow touched by the idea of a younger Lexi trucking along in the woods behind her dad, stuffed animals secured away in her backpack.

"You were close to him, weren't you?"

After a long, quiet moment, she said, "Yeah. Yeah, we were close."

"What about your mom?"

Her response was a scathing snort. "My mom. I don't even know where to start on my relationship with her. She… tolerated me. After a while, I realized she'd never really love me, and I just kept my head down around her."

There was an odd note of pain in her voice, and I wanted to pull her to a stop, get to the root of it. I was terrible when it came to talking about personal shit, though. I had no idea where to start, or if she'd even welcome any questions I might ask.

"I was close to my parents," I said, the words coming almost reluctantly. "I can't imagine growing up with parents who weren't…" I fumbled, unable to figure out where to go from there.

"It wasn't that bad." She had to duck under a low-hanging branch. "Mom resented me, but Dad loved me. I just learned to go to him when I needed things or if there was something I wanted to do. He was a good dad. He pretty much made up for me having a mother who sucked."

"When did they divorce?"

She stopped and looked back at me, head cocked. "They didn't."

I was confused now.

Lexi hitched up a shoulder. "Mom and Dad had initially wanted to have a big family, fill a house with boys and girls. But there were complications while she was having me. The doctors made it clear that I'd be the only child she could have."

I waited for her to go on.

Instead, she just turned around and resumed walking. "The creek is just ahead."

I could hear it. But I had lost interest in the hike. Moving to catch up with her, I caught her arm and tugged until she looked back at me. "Are you telling me she resented you because she couldn't have other kids?"

"Pretty much." She gave an easy shrug, and her pretty gray eyes held mine with little to no sign of emotion.

But I didn't believe it. There was hurt lying underneath that cool, tough exterior. I could practically feel it.

"She was wrong."

Lexi's lashes swept down.

I closed the distance between us, the toes of my boots touching hers. Reaching up, I cupped her chin and guided her head up until she was once more looking at me.

"She was *wrong*," I said again, making sure she heard the intensity in every word.

"I know that." She offered a sad smile, then leaned in and kissed me. She was gone in just a blink.

The feel of her mouth on mine was enough to make my brain start to melt, but I focused on her voice as she continued to speak. "She was wrong, and I know...and it's okay. I've dealt with it. She sends me a card on my birthday and at Christmas. I do the same, and one on Mother's Day. Sure, it's not a great relationship, but it is what it is."

"It *shouldn't* be like that."

She finally looked back at me. "No, it shouldn't. But I figured out a long time ago that life isn't fair – that sometimes life gives you some shitty stuff to deal with and you can either piss and moan about it or accept it and move on."

I moved to her and covered her cheek with my hand. "I'm sorry."

"Don't be." She placed her hand over mine and squeezed lightly, then let go. "Come on. Let's check out the creek and see what we're going to be doing next."

THE CREEK WAS A BUST. Both of us found spots where we thought there *might* have been traps, but there was no sign of anything else, not even tracks that we could follow in hopes of maybe locating the poachers' camp.

They had to have one. It had been quite a hike to get to the spot where that snare had injured Lexi. It didn't make sense that they'd leave the relative privacy of the woods via the main trailhead. It was too exposed, and there was too much of a chance of discovery, either on their way in or way out.

It made more sense that whoever was doing it had a base camp somewhere remote, someplace that wasn't as likely to catch attention. It was entirely possible they'd have somebody coming out to meet them. If vehicles were left in one spot in the park for too long, it was bound to catch attention, so it made sense to me that the poachers probably had somebody else helping them out.

An idea danced in the back of my mind, and I considered it, then tucked it away. It was worth exploring, but not now.

Up ahead of me, Lexi stopped in the middle of the trail. It forked right in front of her, and as I drew even with her, I saw a despondent look on her face. "Nothing."

"We might have to give it a couple of trips out before we find anything," I said, covering her shoulder with my hand. "Maybe they heard you'd gotten hurt and pulled out for a little while. It would be the smart thing to do."

"I've considered that." She made a face. "And if that *is* the case, then more than likely, it's somebody who is affiliated with the park or the SAR groups. The typical poacher coming in here isn't going to be aware of everything that's going on, especially not one ranger tripping and hurting her ankle."

"You didn't *trip*. You got caught up in a snare. There's a difference."

She rolled her eyes. "*I* know that, but the snare effectively tripped me." She hooked her thumb around the strap of her pack, staring out into the trees with a brooding expression. After a few minutes, a soft smile bloomed across her lips. "You know, the first time I hiked out this far, I was fourteen. Dad and I spent a weekend out here, just me and him. We sat up until it was probably almost midnight and Dad told me ghost stories. I was almost too scared to go to sleep."

"You miss him."

She nodded wordlessly. She slanted a look over at me.

"You know, I've done a lot of talking about my family. But other than what you told me about Ryan, I know next to nothing about you."

I started to tell her there wasn't much to say but realized that wasn't fair. She'd talked easily, openly about her father and had even confided in me about the problems with her mom.

I stared off at nothing for a long time, trying to coax my tight throat into relaxing.

"My parents were killed in an accident back when Ryan and I were still in school." Memories of that rainy, cold night danced through my mind. "We'd just won the regional football championship. They were in a car behind us – Ryan and I had wanted to ride the bus with our teammates." Closing my eyes, I took a deep breath, then looked back at her. I never talked about my family. It was surprising how easy it was to open up to Lexi. "We were on this narrow, two-lane road. The bus driver saw the car coming – the driver was drifting over the lane. He honked at the guy, but…"

She linked her fingers with mine. The simple act of comfort caused a lump to form in my throat. I tightened my hand around hers just slightly, still staring into the trees. "The driver ended up drifting over the line again, but the opposite one. He was about to go off the road when he overcorrected and went smashing in the car my parents were driving. They were driving fifty-five, and the cops suggested the evidence pointed to him driving over seventy. They all died on impact."

"I'm sorry, Roman." She leaned her head against my arm.

I nodded. The phrase so often seemed trite, empty, even when people truly meant it. But I took comfort in hearing it from her. Maybe because she knew what it was like to lose somebody.

"Anyway." I cleared my throat. "Ryan and I went to live with my dad's mother. She was older and didn't really know how to handle two grieving teens, but she did her best. She died not long after we turned twenty-one."

"So, it's just you now."

"Yeah."

She moved to stand in front of me, leaning against me. The packs kept us from really being able to embrace, but she rested a hand on my hip just below the sturdy strap that secured the lower half of my pack, balancing the weight of it.

I curved a hand over her neck and pressed my lips to her brow. I lost track of how long we stood there like that.

She was the one to pull away, looking up at me with an expression of tenderness so complete, it made my chest ache.

I was falling for this woman, and I was falling fast.

A few months ago, the idea would have terrified me, but although I *was* scared, everything with Lexi felt incredibly right.

"We should start heading back," she said, her voice husky.

I nodded, but instead of turning around, I lowered my head and pressed a soft kiss to her lips.

This tough, mouthy woman had gotten under my skin.

We broke apart, and I stepped aside, gesturing for her to lead the way. She was more than capable of handling these woods, and it was clear she knew her way around them far better than I did.

Still, I couldn't push aside the nagging worry I'd been carrying with me ever since I realized she was out searching for evidence of the poachers.

I made up my mind, then and there, that I'd take care of her.

It was a need that burned inside me, and I wasn't about to ignore it.

While I knew Lexi was more than capable of handling herself out here in the woods, and in other areas, I couldn't banish the urge inside me, one that insisted I look out for her.

We barely knew each other, and up until the night Cass's plane had gone down, I hadn't even been aware that Lexi existed.

And it didn't matter.

I was going to watch out for her.

I couldn't stand it if something were to happen to her.

ABOUT HALFWAY BACK TO THE TRAILHEAD ENTRANCE, I TOLD Roman I wanted to follow a different trail, one that would cover a more rugged bit of territory. There was still a trail, but like the one that had led to the ranger cabin, this one wasn't used much.

I saw evidence of black bears in the area and started to move more slowly, although my mind wasn't entirely on the task. I kept thinking about Roman – recalling everything from the tense moments when we'd first met to how he'd squeezed my hand earlier when telling me about his parents.

There were feelings blooming inside me that I couldn't even begin to define. I wasn't any good at it. I'd only had one semi-serious boyfriend, and that had been early on in my college career. I'd been going for a double-major at the time, and he was pushing for more and more of my time. It hadn't been all that hard for me to end it, telling him that I needed to focus on college at that moment.

I realized that I could barely even remember what he looked like and found myself laughing to myself.

"What's so funny?" Roman asked behind me.

"Nothing." I continued to smile, but it faded as I thought about what my thoughts might be like in a couple of years. Would memories of Roman fade as fast as they had with my college boyfriend? I couldn't even begin to imagine forgetting about Roman – forgetting *anything*. Even if once this was over, we never saw each other again, I couldn't imagine not having the thoughts of him that blazed so brightly fade, not even a little.

Something on the trail caught my eye, and I forced my thoughts back to the matter at hand.

"What's that?" Roman asked behind me as I crouched in front of a fallen tree. It had fallen a long, long time ago and another younger tree was struggling to grow in the empty space its death had provided. It was maybe up to my hip, branches spreading out. The first spring buds hadn't even started to open.

What had caught my attention was thick, sticky-looking and so dark brown it looked black.

I wrinkled my nose when I recognized what I was looking at. "Chewing tobacco. Gross."

I rose to my feet and looked around, brooding. I didn't see any sign, other than that disgusting mess, that anybody had been on the trail in the past few hours. But one thing was sure.

"Whoever decided to go spitting that nasty stuff onto my trail, they were here *after* the snow. Otherwise, it wouldn't still be hanging there like that."

Roman came around me and crouched down, balancing

on his heels without any sign of wobble, never mind the big, heavy pack he was carrying. He leaned in, getting a lot closer to that mess of nasty, chewed-up tobacco than I'd get. "After the snow, yeah, but it's not super-fresh either. Doubt they were out here today," he said, rising back up to his feet with smooth, easy grace.

I made a face. I didn't want to know how he knew that, but some evil, twisted bit of curiosity had me asking, "Why do you say that?"

"It's not wet. So the dumbass spit it out some time ago."

"Oh." I hadn't even thought of that. The only reason I'd recognized it as tobacco was because a friend of my dad had liked to chew. He'd always spit it into a can when he was around us, but I'd been around him enough to know what I was looking at.

"Not sure if this means we're on the right track or not," Roman said, turning to face me. He rubbed the back of his neck as he lifted his eyes to study the sky. "But we don't have time to keep on looking unless you plan on camping out again."

"No." I shook my head. I wanted a hot meal and a shower. I loved being out in the mountains, but if I had actually planned on *camping*, I would have been better prepared.

"Okay." He went to turn.

Without thinking about it, I reached out and caught his arm. "Roman...thank you."

"For what?" He gave me a perplexed look.

"For being out here with me. For wanting to help." It had been a long time since I'd even wanted to *trust* somebody to help me out. But I was beginning to trust Roman. Leaning in, I pressed my mouth to his.

It was meant to be a sweet, easy kiss.

But it changed — *fast*.

He'd gone to stroke his tongue along my lower lip, and I opened, sucking him into my mouth. He stiffened, then I found myself being backed up until my pack came into contact with an immovable object. One of the big trees that that towered over us.

He reached between us, and I was caught off balance when the weight of my pack suddenly shifted. He'd freed the chest strap, then the harness that held it secure at my hips. Before I had to do much more than shift my weight, he eased the pack off me and dropped it to the ground next to us.

Then he was leaning into me.

As he pushed his knee between mine, I groaned, stepping to spread my legs apart to accommodate the hard, heavy length of his thigh. He caught my hips and dragged me in closer. I whimpered and wiggled, arrows of heat already shooting through me and centering down in my pussy.

"Roman," I whispered. The need I had for him laid me low.

He eased back and stared down at me, eyes hot and hungry. "I can't get enough of you."

"Good." I caught him around the neck and tugged his mouth back down to mine.

One hungry, drugged kiss led to another. I'd never gotten so aroused from something as simple as *kissing*. But there was nothing simple about Roman's kisses. They were deep, delicious and dark, a seduction in and of itself and I was probably already addicted.

Something brushed against my belly. The muscles clenched, and I gasped as I realized it was his hand.

He pulled back and stared down at me as he slid his hand down and cupped me through my sturdy khaki cargo pants. I gasped as he started to rub me, grinding the heel of his hand lightly against me.

"If we had the time, I'd strip you naked and take you here," he murmured, lowering his head to kiss my neck.

I tried to ignore the punch of heat those words caused. It didn't work. In an effort to cool my sudden desire to demand he do just that, I tried to think of reasons why that was a bad idea. "Mosquitoes."

He grinned at me. "Not this early in the year."

"Bears."

"They wouldn't come around once I had you busy screaming as I filled you with my dick."

My knees wobbled.

"Got any other excuses, Lexi?"

I squeezed my eyes closed.

He kissed my brow. "I'm not going to strip you naked out here, Lexi."

He continued to grind the heel of his hand against my clit, and I pressed my face against his chest, so he couldn't see the disappointment. He increased the pressure, and I whimpered, already losing myself to the need. I was already wet. I could feel my panties sliding back and forth over sensitive tissues, and the sensation just made everything worse – or was it better?

"Please," I said, gasping.

"But what about the bears?" he teased, his lips pressed to my ear.

"Bears?" I asked, my foggy mind already forgetting what I'd said only a minute earlier.

He lifted his head and stared down at me.

Something flashed in his eyes, and he stepped back.

I reached for him with a whimper.

But all he did was strip out of his pack and put it on the ground next to mine. Then he pulled me against him once more, one arm banded around my waist.

He popped open the zipper of my khakis.

I gasped in response when I felt his fingers stroke over my belly, then lower, lower, lower.

When he found my clit, my hips jerked involuntarily, pushing against him in a silent, instinctive plea for more.

He gave it to me too. Strange, tight little noises escaped me as he pushed two fingers inside my cunt, curling and stroking. He let go of my waist, and I wobbled, reached for the trunk of the tree at my back. He nudged my pants down to just below my hips, then he slid his arm back around me, protecting the soft flesh of my bottom from scraping against the rough bark behind me.

With his free hand, he started to stroke me again, faster, rougher. He kissed me, his tongue echoing the rhythm of his fingers.

I completely forgot about everything but him – his mouth, his fingers as they so skillfully worked my body, the heat of his body as he caged me in, the strength of his arm around my waist.

"Come for me, princess," he said against my mouth.

I whimpered. If I could have managed to speak, I would

have told him there wasn't much choice in the matter – my orgasm was already racing at me and trying to stop it would be like trying to stop a flood.

My knees wobbled, and I felt the strength draining out of me. My body had gone all liquid and loose, except for a few specific points – my nipples were tight and aching as they stabbed in my bra. My pussy was wet, and the muscles down low inside were clenching as I started to work myself against him, chasing after the climax.

It wasn't much of a race.

Roman twisted his wrist, then scissored his fingers inside me, and I tore my mouth away from his, a sharp, high scream escaping me.

He smothered it against his mouth.

My skin felt too tight, too small, to hold everything breaking apart inside me. Then I went flying... flying...flying.

As I started to drift back down, my awareness returned.

Roman's chest was moving with his hard, ragged breaths. His body was locked and tight, and I wasn't sure, but I thought he might be shaking.

Then I realized there was no *might* about it.

Roman was quivering. I slid my hand between us and cupped his cock through his jeans.

He immediately caught my wrist. "No," he said, voice raw. "It's not a good idea for me to go getting that distracted in the open like this."

He pulled back. I saw a muscle clench in his jaw, then slowly relax.

"What do you mean?" I asked as he reached down and

tugged my pants back up, fumbling a bit with the button, then dealing with the zipper.

He waited until he was done to answer.

"I mean, for all we know, somebody heard us. What if it was one of the poachers?"

We could easily claim we were just hiking, but I saw his point. My face flushed as I realized how stupid this had been.

"Don't," he murmured, pressing his mouth to mine. "Don't go regretting anything we did. I was...mostly keeping an eye on things."

I mustered up a smile. "Is that something you learned being a Ranger?"

He shrugged, then dropped a kiss down on my forehead. "Come on. We need to get back before it's too dark."

"I NEED TO STOP BY THE VISITOR'S CENTER ON THE WAY out," I said, looking over at Roman as he hefted up my pack and put it in the backseat of my Jeep. If I was honest, I'd admit that I didn't really *want* to stop by the visitor's center. I wanted to go home and soak in a tub and drink a glass of wine, then sleep for a week. My muscles were killing me, and although my ankle had held up pretty well, it ached dully and let me know that I had definitely pushed things too hard.

"Why?"

"I'm probably hoping against hope, but I want to see if Hawthorne has made a decision about whether or not I can come back to work. Tomorrow is supposed to be my day to work." A dull ache settled in my chest. Although for the most part of the day, I'd been otherwise occupied with either the search or the sex, I'd spent more time than I liked worrying about my job.

I didn't *like* worrying.

It seemed to be a useless pursuit. Worrying didn't *change* anything.

But this one time, I couldn't make myself stop.

I was *scared*. I couldn't stand the thought of losing my job. This was my dream job, what I'd wanted my whole life. When I'd been a kid, my dad would bring me out here, and I'd pretend to be a forest ranger who came to rescue him after he got hurt while out camping. A melancholy cloud settled around me, and I swallowed the knot in my throat.

Something clued Roman into some of the shit tangled inside me, and he moved in close, pulling me up against him.

He held me like that for a long moment, and I sighed, leaning into him and taking comfort in his solid presence.

"It's going to be okay," Roman said.

Instead of answering, I just snuggled in close and closed my eyes. I so wanted to believe that.

But I wasn't going to count on it either. I was just going to wait and see what happened.

"I'll follow you down," he said. He hesitated, then brushed my hair back. "Maybe you'd let me buy you dinner once you're done."

I looked down at my sweaty, wrinkled clothes then met his eyes. "Dressed like this?"

"You look beautiful to me."

My face flushed at the unexpected compliment, and I bit my lip, hiding a shy smile. "I think I'd like dinner. I know a few places around here that won't care if a couple of tired hikers drop in for a burger or something."

"Sounds good to me." He kissed me again, then nudged me toward the car. "I'll meet you at the welcome center."

THE THOUGHT of sitting down with a burger and Roman had replaced my fantasy about lounging in a tub of hot water, although I just might still have that hot bath. It would just be a little later than planned.

He followed along behind me as I took the winding mountain road that led back to the visitor's center.

Once we got there, we both parked in the corner. He was out of his truck before I'd managed to do much more than unbuckle my seat belt. My muscles felt like they'd been replaced with wet cotton batting and my bones had turned to lead. Before climbing from the Jeep, I dug out a bottle of ibuprofen, but it was empty.

He was waiting for me next to my vehicle and gave me a thorough, head-to-toe look as I carefully eased my feet down onto the pavement. Muscles in my thighs screamed at me, and I couldn't keep from grimacing as they protested.

"Sore?" he asked softly.

"Very." I braced a hand on the car and carefully rotated my left ankle. It was tight, but other than that persistent ache, it didn't really hurt. I'd have to elevate and ice it for a little while, though. Just to be sure.

Wearily, I shifted my attention to the visitor's center, then scanned the parking lot. I didn't see Hawthorne's vehicle, but sometimes he rode with his wife. She worked in town and would pick him up on the way home. It was probably wishful thinking, but I really wanted to talk to him and see if they'd come to a decision about everything.

Part of me also wanted to bring up the subject of poaching, but I wasn't sure if I was ready to do that without proof.

They'd already gone to look for the snare and hadn't found anything. I think Hawthorne liked me, but that didn't necessarily mean he was going to believe me about possible poachers. That idea rubbed me wrong too. There had been enough problems with poaching in the parks that it wasn't a far-fetched idea.

I could still hear Stilwell's smug voice as he suggested I'd made up a story about a snare to try and get out of trouble.

Asshole.

Maybe that was *his* way of dealing with problems, but I didn't lie my way out of things.

"You looked pissed," Roman said, voice neutral.

We were halfway across the lot, just behind the front row of cars, and I stopped to look up at him. "Do I?"

"Well, not so much now, but a few seconds ago…yeah. What's wrong?"

"I…" I almost told him nothing, but then, with a hard sigh, I said, "I'm brooding about whether my boss might believe Stilwell's garbage."

"I'll say something to him," he offered again.

If it came to it, rather than lose my job, I'd probably let him step up, but for now, I wanted to find the proof of the poachers and deal with it that way.

"Thanks," I said, taking his hand and squeezing. "But not yet. Let's look around for a little longer. If Hawthorne *does* believe me, there's going to be a big search for them, and who knows, maybe that will spook them. I don't want them *spooked*. I want them *caught*."

"Okay."

We walked inside together, and I gestured toward the back. "I'm going to take care of a few things. Wait for me?"

"You bet."

I left Roman behind, perusing the public area while I headed into the back. It wasn't Hawthorne's evening to supervise closing up, but I hoped maybe he was still here. Sometimes, he stayed later than scheduled to deal with all the responsibilities he had.

But the door to his office was shut, and no light shone from under it.

"Hey!"

I looked up as Amy rounded the corner. She stopped rolling her chair and rested her hands on the armrests, looking at me with a bright smile. "I've been missing you around here," she said.

I went over and bent down, giving her a quick hug. "Miss you too. I was hoping to talk to Hawthorne. Have you seen him?"

"He's already gone for the day," Amy said, shaking her head.

Disappointment welled, but I pushed it down. "Are you closing tonight?"

"Yeah." She made a face at me. "With Stilwell."

"Oh, lucky you," I said sympathetically.

"Yeah, I got all the luck...mostly bad."

"We all have to take our turn dealing with that...person."

She smothered a laugh. "Nice cover there."

She signed something at me, and I grinned at her. Amy worked with a group of disabled kids in Estes Park, and a couple of them were deaf. She was teaching me some sign on the side, and she'd just called Stilwell an asshole.

"So agree," I told her.

"I better get back out front before he comes looking for me," she said glumly. "Hurry back, okay?"

She wheeled off, and I tried to take comfort in the fact that she seemed to think I *would* be coming back.

If I'd been fired, wouldn't they have heard something?

I had no idea.

Suddenly, I wanted to be out of there, tucked away in a battered booth with Roman, a big, messy burger in front of me. "Check the schedule, then, and get on out of here," I muttered.

I headed into the kitchenette area. They kept a schedule posted on the bulletin board. If my name wasn't marked out, I'd come in and hope for the best.

I didn't notice the scrap of paper until I'd almost stepped on it.

Grumbling about people who couldn't clean up after themselves, I stooped to pick it up. The tired muscles in my thighs and back *screamed* at the movement, and I decided the first order of the evening would be to take some ibuprofen.

I closed my fingers around the small white note and groaned as I straightened. Yes, definitely ibuprofen. Maybe a hot bath once I got home.

Absently, I glanced at the note.

There was a series of numbers and letters scrawled across it in a familiar hand. Stilwell had the worst habit of leaving me annoying notes telling me that I'd forgotten to do this, or did I remember to check that, so I could recognize his writing from a mile away. Feeling petty, I started toward the trash, ready to throw it away, but then I stopped and studied the script on it.

I hadn't noticed it right away, but I could see it now, clear as day.

It was a series of coordinates, like what we'd use to locate a place using a map or GPS.

On the margin, in small, cramped writing there were a few more numbers, but they were too short to be coordinates. Dates, maybe?

"What is this?" I muttered.

"Talking to yourself, Alex?"

Without giving it any serious thought, I folded my hand around the note before I turned to face Stilwell. He was giving me a smug look. One of these days, I was going to risk it and knock that smug look right off his face.

"Well, there's nobody better around here I could talk to," I said easily, lowering my hand. Casually, I slid it into my pocket, hiding the note. "Did you want something?"

He gave me a cool, assessing glare. "I thought Hawthorne told you not to come into work until he talked to you."

"I'm not *at* work. I'm checking the schedule. I'm supposed to work tomorrow, and I was going to see if Hawthorne wanted me to come in."

Stilwell gave me a dismissive look. "If you'd ever answer your phone, you'd know. He called and left a message for you at your house. Yes, you're working tomorrow." A faint smile appeared on his face. "Not with me, though. Some other poor sucker has to do with you."

"My heart breaks," I said, voice deadpan.

Something that might have been irritation flickered in his eyes. "Hope you don't go and fuck things up like you did this time, Alex. You might not have a job to come back to, you know."

I resisted the urge to flip him off.

It wouldn't serve any purpose but to let him know he'd gotten to me.

"I appreciate the concern," I said with mock sweetness.

The lines around his mouth tightened. He moved farther into the room, walking around, eyes scanning the tables and floors.

"Lose something?" I asked.

"Just making sure the area is clean before we head out." He met my eyes. "That is part of the job, right?"

I almost laughed. He *never* bothered to take care of his share of the work when it came to keeping our area neat and orderly. There were times when he even left his lunch trash all over whatever table he decided to use. I didn't point that out, though. I was more interested in the way he kept looking around. He was definitely looking for something.

Without thinking, I slid my hand into the pocket and touched the note, wondering.

He gave up on whatever it was he was trying to find and shifted his attention to me. "Come on." He gave me the saddest attempt at a polite smile I'd ever seen and gestured for the door. "I'll walk you out. We're locking up soon."

I didn't point out to him that I knew my way out – and that I knew what time the visitor's center shut down. I just wanted to be away from him.

He shadowed me through the short hallway and out into the main area.

Roman looked up at me from across the room with a

smile. That smile faded as he caught sight of the man at my back.

Stilwell muttered something under his breath, then said, "Stay out of trouble, okay, Lexi?"

My mouth fell open when he said that – *Lexi* – but when I turned to look at him, he was already pushing back through the employee door.

Curious, I tightened my fingers around the scrap of paper, then pulled it out and tucked it into one of my Velcro pockets where it would be more secure.

I'd look at it again when I wasn't likely to see Stilwell.

It was probably nothing, but then again, if it was nothing, what did it matter if I wasted a few minutes trying to figure it out?

It wasn't like I'd be *hurting* anybody, right? If it was what Stilwell had been looking for, I might possibly *inconvenience* him, and some small, petty part of me delighted in the thought.

I took a deep breath, reminding myself it was probably nothing more than trash.

Lexi groaned as she slid out of the booth.

I gave her a sympathetic look. I'd spent enough time working myself to exhaustion to know how much she must be aching. The hike through the mountains had left me tired, but I'd felt much worse. I'd been on missions where I had to move twice as fast, carrying almost double the weight, all the while getting by on just a few hours of sleep, grabbed here and there.

She caught sight of my expression and grimaced. "Sorry. I'm just aching all over. I know I've been mostly off my feet for the week, but that shouldn't make me this sore all because I spent the day hiking."

She reached out and caught my hand. The gesture caught me by surprise, but I schooled my features, so it wouldn't show.

"You maybe want to come over to my place?" she asked, her voice a study in practiced calm.

We'd just pushed out through the doors of the pub where we'd chosen to eat. Now, outside in the cool air, I turned to look at her, not quite able to hide my surprise this time.

The lights coming from the pub were bright enough that I could see the pink flush spreading up her cheeks.

"I'll be honest, Lexi...if I come home with you, it's going to result in me spending a good hour between your thighs. You up to that?"

Her mouth parted, and her pupils expanded until just a thin rim of gray showed. "Yes," she whispered, her voice husky. "I'm definitely up for that."

I wanted to kiss her right there but held back as a couple with kids walked by, all of them in varying stages of exhaustion. Forcing myself to step back, I said, "Let's get a move on then."

I followed Lexi to her place, a cute house tucked away from the road. A heavy growth of trees provided privacy, keeping the building out of sight until after the bend in the drive.

Her porch light was on, as well as one light from inside the house. Everything around us was quiet.

"Nice place," I told her as I joined her on the sidewalk.

"Thanks." She glanced at me. "I've only been here about a year. Lived in an apartment for a few months after college while trying to find a place."

We walked silently to the door, and when she tugged her keys from her pocket, I held out my hand.

She hesitated only a moment before turning them over, the house key already separated from the rest.

"I'll need to disarm the system."

I glanced at her as I fit the key to the lock. "Ever had problems out here?"

"Not since I moved in here, but back when I was living in the apartment, there were two attempts at a break-in. It made me kind of paranoid."

I liked the fact that she'd taken measures to protect herself. I felt oddly protective of her, an instinct that was getting stronger with every passing hour we spent together.

Once we were inside, I waited by the door as she moved over to the wall and punched a code into the small white panel there.

It beeped, and Lexi turned to me. I moved over to her, hanging the keys on a decorative hook clearly designed for just that purpose.

She backed up a step and braced her hands against the counter behind her, lifting her chin to stare up at me. The light filtered into the room from another, leaving us mostly in shadow. I trailed my fingers along her upper arm then spread my hand open and placed it on her neck. Under my palm, I could feel the delicate arch of her neck and just barely, the rapid flutter of her pulse.

She closed her hand over my wrist and tugged as she eased away from me. "I need a shower, like really bad. Mind giving me a few minutes?"

I almost asked if I could join her but decided I might be rushing it. "Fine with me."

"Thanks." She angled her head toward the other room. "Down the hall past the living room, I've got a guest bathroom, if you want to use it."

After I was alone, I decided to do just that. I had one last pair of clean but wrinkled clothes in my pack, and I went to go grab it. By the time I was back inside the house, I could hear water running from somewhere.

That was all it took for me to start picturing Lexi, naked, standing with her face lifted to the shower nozzle as water rained down on her elegant, excellent body. Now, I wished I *had* asked if I could join her. By the time I was in the guest bathroom, my cock was already aching like a bad tooth. I climbed under the spray, adjusting it so that it was just tepid, letting the temperature cool blood that had already started to heat. It wasn't making much of a difference. Sliding my hand down my belly, I closed it over my cock and stroked, thinking once again of Lexi...naked and wet.

My dick jerked in my hand, hungry and ready for a lot more than just a little self service. But if I took care of myself now, I could spend hours playing with Lexi later.

I stroked myself more roughly, bracing my feet wide apart as I pumped my fist up and down. The head, swollen and distended, disappeared then reappeared as I found my rhythm.

My breath came harder, faster.

Closing my eyes, I imagined it wasn't my fist, but Lexi, on her knees in front of me and sucking me deep into her throat.

My balls drew tight in warning.

A moment later, cum spurted from me to splash down and mingle with the water swirling around my feet. I continued to stroke until I'd emptied myself, although my cock made it clear that this was only a stopgap. The demanding thing wouldn't be happy until it was inside Lexi, in her mouth or snug tight in her sweet pussy.

With a groan, I shoved off the tiled wall at my back and reached for the bottle of shampoo sitting on the built-in shelf.

As I washed, I began to think about Lexi and all the dirty things I wanted to do to her.

AFTER BUNDLING up my things and shoving everything but my clean shirt into the pack, I left the bathroom. I put the pack by the front door, leaning against the wall. I dropped my shirt on the back of the couch and followed the faint sounds coming from the other part of the house.

I found Lexi's bedroom easily. The lights were on, and the covers on the big bed had been turned down. I stared for a long moment, thinking about Lexi doing that, drawing down the comforter and linens, leaving the bed so it looked like it was just waiting for us. Why in the hell was that such a sexy idea? I didn't know, but it was.

Lexi wasn't in the room, or the bed, and that was the one problem I found with the situation. On the wall at my right, I could see a door. It was partially open, and I moved over, glancing through the gap visible between the door and its frame.

I saw a mirror. And in it, I saw Lexi. She had her foot up on the counter, stroking her hands down, then up. Slowly, I nudged the door open all the way, still staring at her reflection.

She lifted her eyes and met mine in the mirror.

I moved to stand behind her just as she lowered her foot to the ground. She smelled amazing – lavender mixed with something else. Pushing her damp hair out of the way, I pressed my face to the curve of her neck and found the scent was stronger there.

I wanted to eat her up.

Slowly, I raised my head and met her eyes once more. Gripping her hips in my hands, I tugged her back, moving her so that she stood farther out from the sink. Then I nudged her down until she had her elbows braced on the counter's surface.

"Watch yourself," I told her before going to my knees behind her. I cupped the firm curves of her ass and pushed until I had her open in front of me. The tight pucker of her ass, running down to the pink folds of her pussy. She was already wet, and that made me wonder what she'd been thinking about in the shower.

I might have asked, but that would mean waiting even longer to taste her again.

She gasped as I leaned in and found her with my mouth. The angle was different, but that didn't matter. What mattered was the fact that she was all but melting against my face, pushing her hips back against me greedily.

The muscles in her butt and thighs quivered. I could feel the tiny quakes as I fucked my tongue into her cunt.

She cried this time, the sound broken and sweet.

My cock pulsed in demand, but I ignored it.

Working her until she was practically coming apart in my hands, I toyed, teased, and traced the sensitive swollen flesh of her pussy.

As I felt her start to tighten, her orgasm pushing in on

her, I stood up. I already had my jeans open by the time I was on my feet. Arrowing the head of my cock to her core, I flexed my hips and pushed inside. I gripped her hip with one hand. I pushed the other into the wet silk of her hair and tugged, arching her spine up.

I stared at the mirror, watching her eyes go wide, her mouth forming a soft, soundless *o* of pleasure.

The grip I had on her hair forced her spine into an arch, lifting her breasts until they were on display in the most erotic way. Her nipples were tight, puckered. All but waiting for my teeth and tongue.

They'd have to wait though. I wasn't about to break contact with her pussy just then. Not for anything.

She twisted her hips, rocking up onto her toes with each thrust.

"I like watching while I fuck you," I said, the words coming out of me in a guttural tone.

Her cheeks flushed.

"Do you enjoy it too, Lexi?"

She went to nod, but the grip I had on her hair wouldn't let her.

I slowed my thrusts and asked again, "Do you enjoy it?"

"Yes." It was both a whimper and moan, one of the sexiest sounds I'd ever heard.

"Good." I began to move faster, thrusting deep into the slippery wet well of her pussy.

She braced her right hand onto the surface of the sink and began to drive herself back against me, working herself up and down on my prick. I dropped my gaze, staring at where we joined. The sight of my dick, all slick with her honey, was a punch and I slowed my strokes once more.

She mewled and moved faster, my name falling from her lips. "Roman, *please…*"

"Fuck yourself on my dick, Lexi." A groan shuddered around me as her muscles flexed and tightened, gripping me even more tightly. "Shit, that's a sexy sight, baby. Don't stop."

She didn't.

In fact, she began to rock against me more desperately. The slick moisture from her cunt slid down, coating my balls. The wet, raw sounds of greedy sex filled the air.

My control splintered the next time her pussy flexed around me, and I yanked her back against me, pivoting us both away from the sink. Bending my knees into hers, I urged her to the ground until she was kneeling in front of me on her knees and elbows.

I caught her hair again and pulled, hard.

She cried out, the sound one of stark, utter need.

Her back arched in response to my grip on her hair, and I began to fuck her harder, holding nothing back.

A sharp, high noise filled the room. She keened low and wordless and began to come.

But I didn't stop.

Couldn't stop.

Her body started to wilt against the floor, and I grabbed both of her hips to keep her up and open for me.

My own orgasm raged closer, just out of reach, taunting me.

Swearing, I pulled out of her and rose, tugging her up with me. I boosted her up into my arms and carried her into the bedroom.

The bed was a tall one, and when I laid her down and pushed up her thighs, it opened her for me.

I bent and pressed a hot, open-mouthed kiss to her slick cunt, then stood and thrust inside once more. My elbows caught the crook of her knees, pushing her ass up and high. I gripped the snug curve and held her in place.

She started to moan, and I looked up into her eyes, seeing the lambent heat as it took hold of her once more.

Lexi curled her fists into the sheet beneath her, her neck arched, mouth open.

I bent low over her and kissed her hungrily, greedy for so much more than just this.

This, as good as it was, just wasn't enough.

And I didn't know what possibly could *be* enough, not when it came to her.

Lexi pushed a hand into my hair and held on as she opened her mouth for me. She wasn't a passive lover. Her tongue came out and twined with mine, then dipped into my mouth as if she craved my taste as much as I craved hers.

Her nails bit into my shoulders, and her tight nipples dragged across my chest, leaving trails of sensation.

I felt it as she started to climax again. Every muscle in my body had gone taut, hard as a rock, just like my dick. I bit her lower lip then pulled away from her mouth to press my face into her neck. My lungs burned with the need for oxygen, my body using up every bit of reserves it possessed. I started to come only seconds after her pussy had started to spasm, milking me with every pulse of her body.

She drained me, completely. As the climax ended, I stood there, bent over her, all the strength in my body gone.

She curled her arms around my neck and sighed out my name.

My heart clenched inside me.

What in the hell was this woman doing to me?

I RARELY SLEPT EASILY.

Even before things had happened with my brother, too often when I laid down to rest for the night, my brain ran in circles instead of slowing down.

But as I laid there, holding Lexi tucked up against my side, my brain started to go slow and hazy.

Vaguely, I remembered thinking that I just might get a few decent hours of sleep.

Then it was like somebody had just gone and turned off the lights in my head, and I was out.

I was dreaming.

I knew it the second I climbed out of bed and looked around.

"Hey, brother."

I turned and saw Ryan standing in front of me. Where there should have been the back wall of Lexi's room, there was just a heavy bank of white fog. Ryan stood with that fog at his back, and as I met his eyes, the fog started to wrap around him, slowly obscuring him from my vision.

"You're going to be okay," Ryan said.

I glanced back at the bed – or at least I tried. There was just more of the fog, circling around us like a barrier. The space around me was free of it while Ryan, just a few feet away, was practically lost to it.

"You're leaving," I said. Oddly, I didn't feel the deep, sharp pain at the thought of him being gone. There was an ache in my chest, yeah, but there was something else…acceptance.

"Can't stay forever." Ryan crooked a grin at me. "Besides, and excuse the hokiness of the expression, but you know I'm always going to be a part of you. Nothing changes that."

Tears blurred my eyes, and I blinked.

It was just a fraction of a second that my eyes were closed, but when I opened them to look for my brother, there was nothing but that fog around me.

He was gone.

I reached up with the back of my hand and dashed away a tear that had managed to break free.

A soft sound came from behind me, and I turned. This time, through the now-clearing fog, I saw the bed…and Lexi.

I went back to her and slid under the covers. Closing my eyes, I tucked my body up against hers.

The next thing I knew it was morning.

The bed shifted, and I cracked open one eye just in time to see Lexi sit up, her long, naked back to me.

I reached out and stroked a finger down her spine, although my mind was more focused on that weird dream than anything else.

She turned to look at me, then. The sight of her sleepy, sexy smile cleared my head, and I found myself smiling back at her.

"Good morning," she said softly, twisting around and moving closer. She pressed a kiss to my mouth, but before I could deepen it, she was already pulling back.

"Come back here," I said as she slid out of bed.

She turned a laughing face toward me. "I've got to shower and eat. Since it looks like I still have my job, I have to get ready."

I groused under my breath, and she just grinned at me. "I had a good night too, thank you."

She disappeared into the bathroom before I could respond.

I usually hated Wednesdays, especially when I had to work. I always went in later for my shift that day and had to stay to close up. It made for a long, boring day this time of year.

But today, it wasn't getting to me.

I still had a job.

I'd talked to Hawthorne on Monday, and he'd informed me that he'd gone to bat for me, so my job was safe. *Don't do anything stupid like that again, though, you hear me?*

I'd assured him I wouldn't, and that I'd be more careful in the future.

When I'd asked him about the snare, he'd given me a look of frustration and admitted that he'd had several people going out there over the past week and checking that area, plus the surrounding forest, but nobody had found anything.

Then he'd given my hand a quick pat. "If those damn

poachers are at it again, we'll find them, Lexi. Just be patient."

He'd believed me, I realized.

That alone had taken so much weight off my shoulders, I almost felt like I was floating through the day.

I pulled the federally marked Jeep I was using for patrol over to the side of the road and got out. Several cars were there, and a small cluster of hikers stood gathered at a trailhead.

"You guys doing okay?" I asked, moving to meet them.

We talked for a few minutes, and one of the hikers confessed some nerves about the trail they were going to take, so I went back to the Jeep and got out a map.

It was more detailed than some of the ones provided by any of the park's visitor's centers, and waterproofed. We used maps like these on SAR missions, and mine was starting to show signs of wear as I opened it up and put it on the trunk of the sedan closest to the trailhead.

"This is where you're going," I told them, tapping at a spot on the map. "It's an easy enough trail for this area, and when you get there, you'll have a fantastic view of one of the park's waterfalls."

They asked a few more questions, and by the time I had folded the map back up, the girl who'd looked a little less certain now showed signs of excitement.

They all started down the trail, and I returned to my Jeep, map in hand.

I started to climb back in, but stopped, looking down at the map in my hand thoughtfully. An idea formed in my mind, and I went to the back of the Jeep, opening the back hatch.

I found my handheld GPS and a marker that I could later erase from the map's slick surface. Using the folded-down seats as a work surface, I opened the map up.

Digging through my pockets, I found the small sticky note marked with coordinates. Using the coordinates and the GPS, I began my search. By the time I hit the fifth one, I had a bad feeling in my stomach.

Each of these spots were fairly remote areas not often patrolled by the rangers, especially this time of year.

I came to the sixth, and as my eyes located it on the map, I fumbled with my GPS, accidentally dropping it. The rugged device was developed to handle drops and falls with ease, so instead of picking it up to check the function, I continued to stare at the point on the map.

My gut started to tangle in hot, slippery knots as I acknowledged what I'd just found.

It was the area where I'd gotten tripped up by the snare.

I'd swear it was almost the *exact* location too.

Sweat started to break out on my forehead as I continued to mark the locations. Seven in all, and every last one of them were located in an area known to be heavy with wildlife.

There wasn't really *anywhere* in the park that didn't have its fair share of animals, but there were some, like these seven sites, that were particularly known for it.

I squeezed my eyes shut, not wanting to admit to myself what I'd likely found.

But logic, and a slow-burning anger, wouldn't let me dismiss it.

I'd already given some thought as to whether the poachers might have somebody on the inside.

As much as I disliked him, I hadn't wanted to consider that it might be Stilwell.

But this was more than enough to make anybody with a brain suspicious.

ON MY WAY back to the visitor's center, I weighed my options.

The thought of just outright confronting Stilwell wasn't high on my list of choices.

If I was wrong, it would just give him more fuel to use in this stupid vendetta, and he could possibly turn others against me too.

If I was right, he could always just destroy the evidence before I could convince anybody that he was involved.

I couldn't put off doing something, though. Stilwell wasn't working today, and if he was involved, he might be out in the park with the poachers even now.

I decided I'd talk to Hawthorne and see if the two of us could go out and check some of the sites. There was one a few miles farther out than the spot where I'd gotten hurt that seriously had me concerned. If the numbers I suspected to be dates actually *were*, then something was going to happen today at that site.

Once back at the visitor's center, my plan fell apart.

"Hawthorne had to go out to Fall River," Amy said, mentioning the park's newest visitor's center.

"Any idea when he'll be back?"

"Tomorrow." She rolled her eyes. "There's some sort of

meeting with the supervisors – the park superintendent is attending and wants all the hotshots there."

"Damn." I pinched the bridge of my nose, my mind racing.

"Everything okay?" Amy asked.

I forced a smile and nodded. "Just had something I wanted to ask him."

The visitor's centers had free public Wi-Fi, and I found a secluded area where I wasn't likely to be overheard. After connecting to the Wi-Fi, I pulled up my contacts and found the number Roman had just given me Monday morning. While cell phone service was notoriously unreliable out here, some phones could function just fine if there was a solid Wi-Fi connection. I'd made sure I'd have that option when I purchased my latest one.

Roman answered with a gruff, "Hello."

The sound of his voice made my heart flutter. I rubbed the heel of my hand over my chest, trying to pacify the suddenly excited beat I found there.

"Hey, it's Lexi."

"I know who it is," he said. His tone went all dark and sexy, and once more, my heart started fluttering wildly.

"I was wondering if I could ask for a favor."

"Just name it."

"Don't you want to know what it is?" I asked, unable to resist the chance to tease him.

"As long as it doesn't involve me breaking the kind of laws that could land me in prison, I'm all yours."

All mine. I liked the sound of that.

Refusing to melt at the very thought, I cleared my throat

and continued. "I think I might have found the root of the problem. I want to go check it out."

"You're not going alone," he said, his voice hardening.

I rolled my eyes. "Why do you think I'm calling you?"

He was quiet for a couple seconds, then said, "Give me forty-five minutes."

He was gone before I could say anything else, and I checked the time as I lowered my phone.

That should work out just about perfectly.

I was on the clock for another half-hour, and if we made good enough time, we might be able to get to the spot and back before night fell.

THE MOMENT LEXI SHOWED ME THE SCRAP OF PAPER, I KNEW
what it held. I'd seen too many GPS coordinates to not
know when I was looking at another set of them. Tapping
the other series of numbers crammed in next to one partic-
ular set of coordinates, I asked her, "Think they are out
there now?"

"I don't want them to be, but…yeah." She rubbed the
back of her neck, looking down at the map she'd spread out
on the hood of her Jeep. "It makes sense. All of those coordinates point to sites that have high levels of wildlife, especially this time of year."

Tucking my tongue into the corner of my cheek, I
pondered the first site she'd shown me – the one that was
likely marked with today's date.

"We'll have to be prepared to camp out if we're
going out."

"I'm *always* prepared for that." She rolled her eyes. "You
know how many SAR missions could be avoided if people

would just pack basic essentials?" She cocked her head. "Have you got your pack on you?"

"I'm *always* prepared for that." I grinned at her as she smacked at my arm. "Yes, I've got my pack. You want to get on this now?"

"If we don't, I'm worried we'll miss them." She shoved her hair back and gathered it into a ponytail. I knew she'd worked today, but at some point before I'd arrived, she'd changed out of her uniform and into civilian hiking garb. The day was warmer than the previous ones had been, and under the short sleeves of her top, her arms were winter-pale and toned.

"Let's get to it, then."

IT TOOK ALMOST two hours to close in on the site Lexi wanted to investigate.

For the past ten minutes, Lexi and I had been moving in silence, neither of us speaking.

I'd seen the tracks on the faint path, and some searching around revealed a cigarette butt that was still damp on one end. Whoever had tossed it down had passed by sometime recently, and the site couldn't be more than another quarter mile away.

The trees were starting to thin out, and for the past few minutes, the sound of running water had grown increasingly louder.

We were close.

The tree line loomed just ahead, and I gestured for her

to follow me off the path, into the protective cover of the trees around us.

I heard voices now, and judging by the look on Lexi's face, she'd heard them too.

Once I felt we were relatively safe from the risk of somebody in the camp seeing us, I eased around the tree and stared out in the small clearing.

It took only a few seconds to ascertain one simple thing.

Lexi had been right.

We were staring out at the poacher's base camp. There were tents and other various indicators, including what looked like a stone circle for fires. I could see six different men. With the exception of one, they were all dressed in gear designed for hunters, camouflage marked with patterns that resembled leaves and trees.

The one who wasn't in hunting gear was Stilwell, and he stood with his arms crossed over his chest. The clothing he wore was something I called Yuppie Hiker, consisting of khakis and a windbreaker that looked like he'd bought for appearance more than comfort and a backpack that still had that shiny new look to it.

"Look, I know you all aren't happy about this." Stilwell's voice was flat, the tone arrogant.

I glanced over at Lexi, but she had all of her attention focused on the hunters and the asshole who was betraying his badge.

"I'm pretty sure we're in the clear, but we're going to have to avoid a few areas until I'm sure everybody has written this off."

"Why didn't you take that trail to search?"

I couldn't see who had asked it, but he sounded pissed.

"Because that trail wasn't in the grid we planned to search," Stilwell said. It sounded like he was talking through clenched teeth. "The stupid bitch went off with some nutjob, and they were operating on their own."

"Then why the hell ain't she been fired?"

It was yet another new voice. I'd already memorized their positions, and as I took in the very hostile attitudes of the men, I touched my hand to the gun I'd tucked into a holster at my side. I was hotter than hell because I'd decided to opt for discretion and had covered my t-shirt, the holster, and the weapon itself with a flannel shirt that was definitely too heavy for the current temperature.

If I had to draw that weapon, it meant things were getting ugly, and I really wanted to avoid that.

Lexi shifted next to me, and from the corner of my eye, I saw her aiming her phone in the direction of the men and the base camp. We'd already discussed what we'd do if we found them, but still, I was nervous and all but held my breath as she took several shots.

When she put the phone away, I breathed a sigh of relief and jerked my head, indicating we needed to fall back.

We didn't move directly to the trail, making our way through the underbrush instead.

It was harder to be quiet, and that had us moving slower than I liked.

We were almost in the clear when a man appeared in front of us.

He had a roll of toilet paper in one hand. In the other, he held a gun.

Of all the *fucking* luck.

Some guy goes out to take a shit, and we had to stumble across him.

He immediately jerked the gun up. Although I was damn fast with a weapon, mine was still in its holster.

The roll of toilet paper fell to the ground. His gaze flicked from Lexi to me, then back.

"You're the dumb bitch that got tripped up by my snare," he said, voice calm.

Lexi didn't respond.

"That's you, right?" He raised the gun menacingly, and I watched as he leveled it right at Lexi's head.

I wanted to charge him, right then, right there.

But it took only a second to pull the trigger. Rushing him would take far more. Even if I crossed the distance between us in under ten seconds, it would be nine seconds too late to save her.

For the same reason, I couldn't risk pulling my weapon.

Slowly, I moved forward, placing my body partially in front of hers.

"Who are you?" the poacher asked.

"We're just passing through," I said, even though I knew he wouldn't believe it.

"Yeah, right." He spat a mouth full of tobacco onto the ground, then jerked his head toward the clearing we'd been watching. "Go on out there. You wanted to nose around, so by all means, let me give you the grand tour."

I'D FOUND MYSELF IN STICKY SITUATIONS BEFORE, BUT I knew without a doubt, this was the worst.

I was acutely aware of the man walking along behind us. Not too close, though. I had a feeling he was keeping his distance just in case one of us tried to pull something.

My gut had drawn up into tight knots, and I tried not to let the fear I felt show. I had no doubt it would just amuse the man who held the gun on us.

We broke through the tree line, and all discussion stopped as, one by one, the group of men turned to look at us.

Stilwell was the last.

As grim as the situation was, the look of utter shock on his face was satisfying.

His eyes went ugly and dark, while his face mottled with rage. "What the *fuck* is this?" he demanded, striding up to Roman and me. Unlike the man at our back, Stilwell didn't stop until he was almost close enough for me to reach out and touch him. And if I could *almost* do it, I had no doubt the silent man at my right *could* do it.

Stilwell was either more stupid than I realized, or more arrogant. I wasn't sure which.

Neither Roman or I spoke, and Stilwell, his face contorted with anger, snapped, "Well?"

"Roman and I decided to go for a walk," I said blandly.

"Bullshit," the man behind me said. "They've been spying on us."

I didn't respond.

"Who the hell knows you're out here?"

"Your boss, Hawthorne," Roman said before I could even figure out how to respond – or if I should.

The group of men was suddenly gathered around us in a loose circle, all of them talking at once.

I sidled closer to Roman.

I was just barely able to hear him as he muttered under his breath, "Follow my lead, okay?"

I had no idea what he meant.

"We can't let them go telling people what they've seen here!" one of the men argued.

The man who had been standing behind us shifted away to join in on the fray, but kept his gaze, and gun, locked on us. "I'm not going to have some mouthy, stupid park ranger go and cause trouble for me, boys. We need to deal with this."

"Deal with it?" That came from the youngest member of the group, and he gave everybody around him a wide-eyed look. "Please tell me you're not talking about what I think you're talking about."

Nobody responded to him directly, and the conversation became more and more heated.

In a lull in the conversation, Roman spoke up.

His words had me balking.

"I know you guys aren't dumb enough to kill a federal employee – *on federally protected* land," he said, although his tone implied he very much believed they might be stupid enough.

What in the hell was he up to?

I was afraid to even consider his motivations, but his softly whispered, urgent demand from just a moment ago stuck with me. Clearing my throat, I said, "It would take a *lot* of stupidity to pull something like that, especially since I told Hawthorne where I was heading and why." I flicked a look to Stilwell and added softly, "Maybe you should be more careful about the notes you leave laying around."

His eyes widened in understanding, but as two of them turned on him, he pasted a confident smile onto his face. "Nice try, Alex. You and me both know the real reason you're here."

"Oh?" I don't know how I managed to speak in such a calm, easy tone when there was a man pointing a gun at me. "And please, enlighten the rest of the group."

"You've been following me." He shrugged, managing a passable attempt at being unconcerned. "You know it's just a matter of time before everybody realizes I was right about you, and you're trying to find a way to throw me under the bus before it's too late."

Wow. The man's ego was *enormous*.

A smirk curled his lips.

I somehow found it in me to laugh. "You think I'm *threat-*

ened by you, Stilwell? Please. A wet, hungry kitten is more threatening to me than *you* are."

His mouth went tight.

The guys around us had started muttering to each other, and several of them were sliding Stilwell assessing looks.

He sensed it because he turned his attention to the one closest to him – the young-looking guy who'd first voiced his unease over *dealing* with us. "Brad come on...you know me. I'm here to protect you guys. You know that."

"Yeah, well, I'm not feeling very *protected* right now," he said, shaking his head.

"We need to just let them go," one of the others said, speaking up for the first time. He was staring determinedly at the ground.

I had no idea if it was an attempt to make it harder for me to describe him or what, but even when one of the others spoke to him, he wouldn't look up.

"Hardy, what the fuck you think they are going to do if we let them go?" the man who'd caught us asked, voice thick with sarcasm. "Think they'll just *forget* what they saw out here?"

"Frank, I don't know, and frankly, I don't give a flying fuck at this point. I'm all for bagging a big moose, but I'm not going to get involved in...whatever it is you're thinking."

"Sounds like at least a couple of you got brains in your head instead of just bullshit," Roman said. His scathing tone made me twitch, and he wasn't even speaking to me. Part of me wanted to tell him to shut the hell up, but I could already see the divide between the men growing wider. "You can't really expect to come out of this without shit sticking to you.

Not with her boss knowing where we are…and what brought us out here."

Stilwell paled, and I looked at Roman from the corner of my eye to see him staring directly at the other ranger.

Stilwell tried to brush it off, laughing, but the sound itself was sharp-edged, either with nerves or anger. "Hawthorne already knows Lexi had a problem with me. She's been lying about me to him for months, and he's caught her at it more than once."

"You are *so* full of *shit!*" I breathed out, sounding almost amazed. "How in the hell do you even manage to walk around with *that* level of shit packed inside you?"

"Before you go digging the hole any deeper, man, you might want to know that I already told your boss that I saw the snare – he knows there's a poacher out here, and he told me he needed time to develop a case, but…" Roman heaved out a sigh, somehow managing to sound almost sympathetic to Stilwell as he added, "But you should probably start doing some serious self-reflection because you're going to be out of a job soon. He knows you're involved in this."

"How the fuck does he know that?" Stilwell demanded, his calm façade falling to pieces around him.

"Because I told him." Roman spoke in a matter of fact voice, like he was discussing the weather, while all around us, the guys started muttering amongst themselves once more. "You think this is the first time I've followed you out here, you dumb shit? I was on your backtrail when you went out on Sunday. And…well, let's just say that I provided Hawthorne with some very interesting photographs."

"Son of a *bitch*," the one called Frank said.

The anger that had been buzzing around us was now directed at Stilwell.

"How the *fuck* did he manage to find us?" It was Brad, the younger guy.

"Did you let him follow you?" The man with the gun aimed at us was no longer watching Roman and me. He'd shifted his attention to Stilwell, and in the next second, unbelievably, he swung the gun away from us to point at Stilwell, a good ten feet away from us.

Roman nudged me.

I sucked in a breath as he took the next moment and lunged, moving faster than any man I'd ever seen.

The gunman's arm swung back toward him, but Roman caught his wrist and twisted. The weapon fell to the ground in the next second, and I watched in disbelief as Roman shifted again, this time bringing his elbow down on the back of the man in front of him.

The poacher went down like a felled oak.

Another one of the men fumbled for his weapon and Roman dipped down, scooping up the gun the tobacco-chewer had dropped and leveled it on the one opposite him, never once breaking rhythm.

The man slowly raised his hands.

Stilwell stirred, coming out of the daze that had settled over him at Roman's sudden, decisive action.

Before he could interfere, I tapped him on the shoulder. When he swung his head around to look at me, I slammed my fist into his nose. His head flew back, and he stumbled over something before falling backward. His head hit the ground, and his eyes rolled into the back of his head.

One of the other men started toward Roman, and I lunged forward, moving fast.

I tackled him, and we both went down. The fall and the suddenness of my attack stunned him, and I used those few, brief questions to grab a rock and clip him across the back of the head. I hoped I hadn't done him any serious damage.

Clambering to my feet, I looked around, braced to find somebody moving toward me.

Roman had effectively disarmed or disabled almost all of them.

I blinked, my brain not quite processing what was in front of me. Four men, including Stilwell, and the other guy I'd tackled lay completely motionless. One was the man who'd been holding the gun on us, while the fourth, nameless poacher lay curled up in a fetal position, clutching his middle.

The other three men had their hands up and watched Roman with wary eyes.

"Think you can find something to tie these clowns up with?" Roman asked, not once looking away from the men in front of him.

I dumped my pack and hunkered down in front of it to start searching.

THE PARK'S LAW ENFORCEMENT RANGERS, ALONG WITH Hawthorne, finally arrived.

Once Lexi had tied them up, using a variety of materials she'd had in her pack, I went around to check each one of them, making adjustments as needed and checking them all for weapons.

Every one of them was carrying, and I made a mental note of who had been carrying each of the weapons. While Hawthorne was talking to Lexi, I singled out the guy who looked to be the superior among the law enforcement rangers and pointed to the weapons I'd stripped from each of the poachers.

He took notes, going back and forth between me and the poachers to get names and identifying information.

Some of them didn't want to talk.

Stilwell, however, was raging, insisting that he had been out here on his own when he came across all of us. He then insisted he had nothing to do with the men and that Alex was out of her mind.

Lexi growled at him. "It's *Lexi*, you douchebag."

"Hawthorne—"

Hawthorne didn't even look up from his notepad as he snapped, "Shut the hell up, Stilwell."

Under his breath, the man muttered, "*Douchebag* is an insult...to douches."

I smothered a smile. Lexi had her hand in front of her mouth, but I suspected she was trying to do the same thing.

"What made you come out here looking for them, Lexi?" Hawthorne finally asked. He glanced at me. "And without following proper protocol."

There was an unspoken *again* that lingered, and I knew I wasn't the only one who heard it.

Before I could come to her defense, she said, "I tried to find you, but you were out at Fall River. I considered waiting for tomorrow, but I thought it wasn't in the best interest to do that."

"Might I ask why?" Hawthorne fixed a penetrating gaze on her.

She didn't so much as blink as she reached into the side pocket on her cargo pants and pulled out the note she'd shown me. "Because of this. I found it in the breakroom. I figured out they were coordinates and dates. One of the dates was for today. I didn't want to risk them deciding to relocate or something else that might make it harder to track them down again."

Hawthorne took the note and skimmed it, then shifted his attention to Stilwell. "This writing looks kind of familiar."

Stilwell must have realized he was trapped, because he looked away, shoulders slumped.

Hawthorne turned his attention back to us and had us go through the whole story again, from top to bottom.

Once we finished, he pointed us over to one of the rangers who'd accompanied him. "Ride with Grainger on the utility cart. You're both going to the hospital to be checked out."

"But—"

"No *buts*, Ranger Evers. I'm ordering you to get checked out, so I can include it in my report." He narrowed his eyes and directed his gaze to me before adding, "And it would… expedite things if the civilian would do the same."

I wanted to argue but figured going along with Hawthorne's politely worded order would make things easier on Lexi. Giving him a short nod, I hefted my pack from the ground and put it on. Lexi was still trying to talk Hawthorne out of the hospital visit so I grabbed her pack and moved to catch her elbow. "Come on. He's just doing his job, Lexi."

WE WERE STILL WAITING in the emergency room when the cops arrived. They had all four of the poachers who'd been injured with them, and they all received a lot of attention as they were seated. One cop went to sign them in, while six others stood to form a perimeter around them.

They were on the far side of the fairly large waiting room, but there was little question as to whether or not we'd been noticed.

Stilwell glared at us balefully.

I gave him a wide smile as Lexi shifted in the seat next to me, grumbling about the pointlessness of coming to the hospital.

I reached over and rubbed her knee. "Hey, it could be worse."

"Yeah?" She sounded cranky, and I looked away from Stilwell to see her sitting in the seat with her arms folded and eyes closed.

"You could be nursing a broken nose like your buddy over there."

Her eyes opened, and she looked around curiously until her gaze landed on Stilwell.

She broke into a bright laugh, her sour mood fading away. "You've got a good point." She covered my hand with hers, her eyes still on the man glaring at us. "I guess I should lighten up. You're right. Things could definitely be a *lot* worse. One of us could have gotten hurt...or worse."

That last part prodded at a sore spot that I'd been trying to ignore.

I wouldn't be able to do it for much longer.

Had she known?

Back while we were at the poacher's camp, had she known that I was terrified something would happen to her?

I had tried to lash down all of the fear, knowing it wouldn't help and it might just make things worse, but I had no idea if I'd managed to conceal it well enough.

She rubbed her hand soothingly over mine, and although I didn't look her way, I had a feeling she was aware of the turmoil inside me.

I turned my hand over and laced my fingers with hers, staring at Stilwell until he finally averted his gaze.

———

LEXI'S NAME was finally called.

She stood up, then listed to the side, sucking in a surprised gasp.

I immediately rose, gripping her arm to steady her.

"What's wrong?" I demanded.

"My ankle went and stiffened up on me," she said. I watched as she gingerly lowered it and put more weight on her foot.

Even when she flashed me a relieved smile, I was reluctant to let her go. I walked alongside her, and at the door, the nurse gave me a sympathetic smile. "You'll have to wait out here for now."

I wanted to argue.

Lexi rose onto her toes and kissed my chin. "I'm fine. Besides, you've got to take *your* turn getting poked and prodded." She rolled her eyes at the last part.

Reluctantly, I let go.

She wagged a finger at me. "I'm doing this. You better go back when you're called, or we'll have it out."

I managed a smile and nodded. "I'll go back when they call me."

After the doors closed behind her, I shifted my attention to the cluster of officers still standing guard around the poachers.

Stilwell's eyes met mine, then hurriedly jumped away.

I paced over and nodded to the cops. "I was there when these guys were caught."

One of them gave me a look from head to toe, then glanced at the bruised and battered men sitting there in handcuffs. Not one of them looked at me. Stilwell, in fact, had developed a rapt fascination with his designer-styled khaki hiking pants.

"Is that a fact?" the officer close to me said. A grin split his face. "I heard it was a lady who clocked one of them."

"Two of them," I clarified. I pointed them out, indicating Stilwell last. He still wasn't looking at me. "Nice shiner you got there, Stilwell. I see *Lexi's* name written all over it."

He finally shot me a look, malevolence now burning his eyes.

I smiled at him. "You're lucky she put you down so fast. If you'd still been on your feet when I got to you, I would have torn you apart."

"You going to let him stand there and threaten me?" Stilwell demanded, shifting his attention to the cop near me. His voice was nasal and thick, thanks to the damage Lexi had done to his nose.

"Didn't sound much like a threat to me." The cop gave him a thorough study, then clicked his tongue. "You're going to be wearing a souvenir from today for the rest of your life. That nose of yours is definitely broken."

Stilwell's face twisted in rage, but only for a moment. He made a move like he was trying to touch his face – it had to be aching like a bitch. But with his hands cuffed behind him, he couldn't do much of anything.

I laughed. I couldn't help it. "I do believe you're right,

officer. Stilwell, every day, for the rest of your life, you're going to look in the mirror and see your not-so-perfect nose, and I hope you think of Lexi every time."

"I'm sure I will," Stilwell said, his voice taut, eyes glittering.

"Probably be a good thing that you're likely to be spending a little while in prison. You know, with hunting on protected property being a federal crime and all. You'll have some time to cool off."

His lids flickered, but some of his normal arrogance showed as he stated, "You're so sure I'm going to prison."

"I'd bet my right nut on it. See…you being a ranger means they're going to hold you to a higher standard. These dumbasses, maybe their lawyers can argue outright stupidity motivated them." I looked at the one who'd held the gun on Lexi and me. A medic had put a temporary splint on his lower forearm to stabilize the break, but it was pretty clear he was still in pain. "And that's a *maybe*, seeing as how all of you were hiding, so you knew you were walking on dangerous ground. But, Stilwell, you don't even have a chance of taking that route. And I'll be there to watch while you're in court. Matter of fact, I'm looking forward to it."

"Fuck you," he said shortly.

I just grinned at him.

Just as I turned, somebody called my name. The same nurse who'd taken Lexi back just moments ago stood there, waiting. She smiled at me. "Looks like you get to go back after all."

I FOLLOWED ROMAN INTO THE SMALL STABLE AND WATCHED with a grin as one of the horses pushed her head out over the railing and neighed. It sounded very much like a reprimand.

After we'd been discharged from the hospital, I'd asked Roman if he'd come home with me, but he'd told me he had to check on his horses. I'd been disappointed, until he took my hand and pulled me closer. "Maybe you could come home with me," he said, the words cautious.

I'd been delighted and was even more so now.

I loved horses, although I didn't ride as much as I liked.

"Aren't you a beauty?" I said to the one closest to me.

"That's Cap – short for Captain America."

"He's beautiful," I said softly, holding out a hand.

"*She* is beautiful," he corrected me.

"Ah." I rubbed the mare's nose, loving the velvety feel of it. She lowered her head and heaved out an equine sigh of pleasure. "Why not Captain Marvel?"

"Ryan and I were nine when our parents bought them for us," he said, sounding a little sheepish. "I wasn't much concerned about shit like that." He nodded at the other horse, a dappled gray. "That poor girl is Hellboy. She was Ryan's."

Sadness tinged his voice, and I watched as he moved over to rub the horse's neck. "You miss him, too, don't you, girl?"

As if she understood every word Roman had said, Hellboy arched her head up, then rested her neck on Roman's shoulder.

It was like they were hugging.

The sight made my heart ache, and I reached up to rub at my chest just as Roman turned around. He caught sight of me and asked, "Are you okay?"

"Yeah." I summoned up a bright smile. "Right as rain."

He looked like he wanted to call me on it, so before he could, I asked, "Why don't you show me how you feed them? I've ridden horses before, but I've never taken care of them."

"Alright." He jerked his head toward the back of the barn. "Come on. Let's go get some feed for them."

As we walked, I asked, "Do you still ride much?"

"No." He caught my hand and squeezed lightly. "They're getting a little too old for it. And..." His voice trailed off.

I rubbed my thumb against his hand. "It makes you miss him even more."

"I *always* miss him more." He let go of my hand and grabbed a big bucket, turning it over to me. "Some days, like our birthday, it's worse than others. But it never goes away."

"No." I'd come to that understanding on my own in the years since my dad passed away. "You just learn to live with it – with that piece of you missing."

He nodded, then, voice gruff, he told me how much feed to put in the bucket, then showed me the feeding troughs. While I was dealing with that, he gave them fresh water.

Cap nudged him with her nose, and he smiled at her.

I turned away and tried to calm my breathing down. It wasn't easy. My emotions were raging in and out of control and had been ever since I'd finally forced myself to relax while we'd been waiting for reinforcements. We were both safe, and the poachers were restrained. I wouldn't call them harmless. Two of them, including the guy who'd discovered us in the trees, had muttered threats and shot us hateful looks the entire time.

But we were safe.

And now with the day behind us and some of the tension melting from my shoulders, other thoughts were making themselves known.

"I'll give you both a good brushing tomorrow," Roman said behind me, his voice closer than it had been.

He rested a hand over the back of my neck as I reached up to swipe my fingers under my eyes.

He saw and cupped my chin, guiding my face up to his. He brushed one tear away, then pressed his mouth to mine. "Let's go inside," he said.

I'd been prepared for him to ask why I was crying, and I was relieved when he didn't.

Inside the house, he sat down and pulled me closer, his

hands around my hips. He guided me until I stood between his legs, then he pressed his face against my belly and wrapped his arms around me.

A shudder went through me, hard and fast, and I curled my arms around his neck, dipping my head so I could press my lips to his crown.

One of us was trembling. I couldn't tell if it was him or me, and I didn't care.

The impact of everything that had happened, the understanding of how badly things could have gone wrong slammed into me. I sucked in a breath, attempting to calm the storm trying to rise in front of me.

Roman slid his fingers under my shirt and brushed them lightly against my skin. Straightening, I pushed my fingers through his overlong hair and tugged until he lifted his face to mine.

His gaze was hooded, lids drooping low over his eyes. A hungry look crossed his features.

I traced one finger over the curve of his lower lip. He opened his mouth, and I shivered as he sucked my finger into the warm, wet cave, curling his tongue around the tip and stroking me.

I pulled it away and bent down, pressing my mouth to his.

He dragged me into his lap and rubbed his cock against me. I sat straddling him, clinging to the wide shelf of his shoulders. His mouth left mine, but before I could even process the disappointment, he ran his teeth along the arch of my neck.

A rush of goosebumps broke out over my skin, and I shoved my hands into his hair, pulling him in tighter.

"Roman," I whispered.

He pushed my shirt higher, and I caught the hem, dragging it off. Cool air kissed my skin. Inside the cotton of my bra, my nipples pebbled. Roman ran his mouth along the edge of the bra. I groaned and pressed him closer, needing to feel his mouth on me.

His hands slid behind my back, and I felt him tugging at the closure of my bra. It was gone in the next moment, and Roman pressed a hot, open-mouthed kiss to the midline of my body, tracking a path that took him closer and closer to my nipple.

My breathing was already coming hard, and it felt like I could scarcely force enough air through a throat gone tight.

He closed his lips around my nipple, then slowly tugged at it with his teeth. My bones threatened to dissolve on me, the pleasure of his touch blurring my mind.

I rocked against him, wiggling and straining until the length of his cock burned into me. The layers of fabric separating us was far too much. I needed him naked. I needed *me* naked and his cock inside me, stretching and filling me.

I realized only as the last word left my lips that I had spoken out loud.

Roman broke away from my body and caught my hair in his hand, forcing me to meet his gaze.

The hunger burning there all but scalded me, all but melted me. There were suddenly far too many things separating us – my damp panties and wrinkled cargos, his clothing as well. And distance. There were scant inches between us, but he wasn't touching me the way I needed him to touch me, and it felt like miles.

"I'm already on a hair-trigger, Lexi," he said, voice raw and guttural. It stroked over my skin like whiskey-soaked velvet. "You keep that up, and you're going to get fucked like you've never been fucked before."

"Do you promise?" I asked, my blood going molten.

Something flashed in his eyes.

Abruptly, he surged upright. Instinctively, my legs went around his hips, and I groaned, rubbing against him as the position forced his cock and my cunt into an up-close and personal sort of pressure.

He grabbed my hips and kept me from moving like that again. "I'm already about to come in my jeans, so stop it."

The idea that he was that close to losing control delighted me, and I would have kept on moving and wiggling if it wasn't for his grip holding me in place.

Something hard pressed against my hips – a table, I realized.

My feet hit the ground, and no sooner had that happened than he was yanking my pants down, leaving them tangled around my ankles. I still wore my boots, but he clearly didn't give a damn as he shoved my panties halfway down my thighs, then crowded up against me.

I felt the naked brush of his cock and I whimpered.

I went to spread my thighs apart, but the pants around my lower legs prevented it.

"Roman–" His name ended on a sob as he spun me around, then thrust inside me, big and hard and thick. He felt deeper somehow, even bigger than normal. I grabbed onto the edge of the table, clinging for purchase as he drove his cock back in, pulling out until only the fat head stretched me, then filling me again.

And again.

And again.

I spasmed around him, and he swore, hands gripping me tight enough that I wouldn't be surprised to see bruises.

And still, he drove into me. Sweat dripped into my eyes, beaded across my skin, and heat suffused my every pore.

He yanked my hips up, pulling them completely off the table. My booted feet left the ground, and now all of my weight was balanced between my upper torso as it rested on the table – and on the cock impaling me.

He swelled, so huge it felt like I couldn't possibly take any more.

A hot, tight knot formed low in my belly, spreading and spreading until all of me was clenched and ready.

Roman muttered my name, and just like that, I exploded, breaking around him and coming hard and fast.

He caught my shoulder in one hand, letting my weight settle once again on the table, then he used his hold on me to yank me back onto his cock, holding me locked in place, completely vulnerable to him.

In the next second, his cock swelled, then jerked, and I whimpered as he started to come.

He sagged forward, shoving out his hands to brace his weight just before he would have dropped completely down onto me.

I moaned and shuddered, my pussy still milking him in desperate demand.

He shoved my sweaty hair away from my neck and kissed me.

"Lexi…"

The dazed satisfaction in his voice was almost as sweet as the mini quakes still wracking my body.

My heart clenched as he settled a hand on my hip and rubbed, the gesture tender and soft.

I had no idea how it had happened so fast, but I'd gotten myself lost in this man.

And I didn't ever want to find my way free.

WATER RAINED DOWN AROUND US.

I leaned against the tiled wall and smiled at Roman as he dipped his head to kiss me. I was completely drained, and when he pulled away, I wrapped my arms around him, snuggling in close, wishing the cast was gone so I could hold him as tightly as I wanted.

"I don't think I can stand on my own," I told him.

"Lean on me all you want," he said.

I tipped my head back to stare at him, unconcerned by the showerhead as it spilled water down on the back of my head. "I think I like the sound of that."

"Is that a fact?" He cupped his hands over my shoulders and dipped his head and rubbed his lips over mine. I clung to his hands and sighed at the sweetness of the moment.

"Yeah." I smiled against his lips. "I've never been much for leaning on anybody but leaning on you doesn't sound so bad."

He slid an arm around my waist and pulled me in closer. "Maybe it will make it easier if I said I wouldn't mind leaning on you too."

We stood there like that, arms wrapped around each

other as the water came down on us. Roman murmured something. It was so quiet I thought maybe I'd misunderstood him.

Pulling back, I looked up at him. "What did you say?"

A dull red flush settled on his cheeks.

I reached up and touched his lips. "What did you say, Roman?"

He pushed a hand into the wet weight of my hair and twisted the strands around his fingers, holding my head in place.

"I think I'm falling in love with you," he said, the words gruff and low, hesitant even.

There was a look of uncertainty in his eyes and my heart just melted.

Reaching up, I cupped his face in my hands, drawing him down to my level.

"Yeah?"

He pressed his brow to mine and murmured, "Yeah."

A sweet satisfaction unlike anything I'd ever felt settled inside me. I curled my arms around his neck and said, "I think I'm falling in love with you too."

His lids flickered, then a slow smile curled his lips, transforming everything about him. He looked younger. He looked...open. "Yeah?" he whispered, echoing my response from only seconds ago.

"Yeah."

"WHO IN THE HELL GETS MARRIED IN DECEMBER?"

Roman laughed as he cut around me, juggling the bags that held his suit and my dress, along with the tote that carried all my makeup. I rarely bothered with makeup, but it wasn't every day that my cousin and one of my best friends got married.

The day of Breanna and Ryder's wedding had arrived. The ceremony was taking place in a few hours, and we had a snowstorm to drive through to get to the wedding location. I eyed Roman's truck through the heavy fall of snow. "You sure you can drive in this?"

"I grew up in Lyons, baby," he replied, his voice easy. "I've been driving in messes like this for more than half my life."

I had too, but at the same time, the near white-out conditions were making me nervous.

Or maybe it was just because of the wedding. Breanna asked me if I'd stand up with her as her maid of honor. I'd never been part of a wedding party in my life. Fortunately, I wasn't going to be up there alone. Breanna, never one to do things the traditional way, was having her friend Stella stand up with her as her matron of honor.

Hopefully, I wouldn't be the one to trip over my skirt as I walked down the aisle.

The thought made me laugh, and I shook my head.

"What's so funny?" Roman asked as he cut around me.

As he put the clothes into the back, I answered, "I was just thinking it's a good thing I'm not going to be up there with Stella alone and how I hoped it wouldn't be me that tripped and fell over my feet. Then I got to thinking about how bad it would be if it was *Breanna* who fell." I heaved out a mock sigh of despair. "I guess if somebody *has* to fall on their face, it's better if it's me. Stella's pregnant and Breanna shouldn't fall on her face on the day of her wedding."

"You're not going to fall on your face," Roman said, turning to me. He held out a hand for the shoe box. I passed it over and opened the passenger door. Before I could pull myself up into the truck, Roman boosted me onto the seat. I bent over and kissed him in thanks.

His mouth lingered on mine, his fingers curving around the back of my neck to hold me in place.

He nipped my lower lip, but before he could take my mouth in one more kiss, I pushed him back. "You keep that up, we'll end up being late."

"It would be worth it." He grinned at me, snowflakes collecting on his lashes.

"Maybe for you," I said grumpily. "You wouldn't have Breanna furious with you."

"Oh, she'd be mad at me too. It's not like you'd be late

over being engaged in…solo pursuits."

I snorted, then playfully pushed at his shoulder. "Come on. I have to be there and hold her hand. She's probably a stressed-out wreck."

BREANNA WAS INDEED A NERVOUS WRECK, but not because I'd been late. We'd made very good time getting to Denver, and I was at the hotel hosting the wedding and reception with plenty of time to spare.

No, the reason for her state of mind was currently on her knees in the suite's bathroom, emptying her stomach.

Breanna hovered by Stella's side, making soothing noises, but I could see the stress in her eyes.

I went into the bathroom and nudged Breanna out of the bathroom. "You, go. Sit. I'll help Stella."

Breanna tried to argue, but I insisted. "The stylist is coming to do your hair in less than twenty minutes. You don't need to be in here while Stella is dealing with morning sickness."

"It's not morning," Stella grumbled behind me. I turned and went to her, rubbing her shoulder. She wore a robe over her bra and panties, and her hair was scooped back into a simple ponytail. As another retch hit her, I caught the long tail of her hair and held it back.

A few minutes later, she straightened and gave me a grateful look. "I think it's over."

I nodded and gestured to the main room of the suite. "I'll go get her calmed down."

"I heard that!" Breanna shouted.

Stella met my eyes and grinned at me, color already returning to her face.

"Good!" I shouted back. "I wanted you to hear it."

She was laughing when I entered the room. As the sound faded, I moved to stand up behind her, resting a hand on her shoulder. She was still staring outside at the gently falling snow. "Talk about a white wedding," she murmured.

I laughed. "Only you could get the weather to go along with you like this."

A knock on the door interrupted us, and I hugged Breanna. "That's probably the stylist."

I MADE it down the aisle without falling.

Both Stella and Breanna made walking in heels look graceful and easy. I was more used to my hiking boots, but I was happy enough to just get to my spot without tripping.

The second the photographer said she was done with the pictures, I kicked my shoes off. Roman came up behind me and slid his arms around my waist. "I was wondering how long it would take for you to do that."

"Hey, I'm proud of myself. I didn't complain about them once." I turned my head and twisted until I could meet his eyes.

He dropped a kiss on my lips.

I turned around and hooked my arms around his neck, no cast getting in the way.

He ran the back of his fingers down my cheek and pressed his thumb to my lower lip. He didn't kiss me again, though. I'd fussed at him earlier for smudging my lipstick, and we'd made a deal. Once the wedding was over, he could smudge it all he wanted.

I was looking forward to it.

The lead singer of the wedding band announced that it was time to welcome the new bride and groom, and we moved over to watch as husband and bride came in. Breanna looked beautiful, her face practically glowing.

Ryder was a quieter presence, but it was obvious he adored the woman he'd married.

I leaned against Roman as the first strains to their wedding song came on. He slid his arm around my waist. Through the satin of my dress, I could feel the heat. Although I was watching my cousin and her husband as they shared their first dance as husband and wife, my attention was on Roman.

As soon as another song started to play, he pulled me into his arms, and we swayed together.

"Are you having a good time?" I asked him.

"I'm dancing with you. How could I not be having a good time?" He pressed the flat of his hand to my back and urged me closer. "You look beautiful. I don't know if I've mentioned that."

I rolled my eyes, although his words definitely pleased me. "You've mentioned...oh, five or six times?"

"That's all?" He arched his brows and shook his head. "I'm slacking."

I laughed and curled my arms around him. My breasts went flat against his chest, and Roman groaned, dropping his head to rest his chin on my shoulder. "You're trying to drive me crazy."

"Maybe." I skimmed my lips across his cheek. As I

looked up, Breanna and Ryder passed by us. Breanna was practically floating. If I looked down and saw that her feet weren't even touching the ground, I don't think it would have surprised me.

The dance ended, and Roman took my hand, guiding me over to the bar. He got a beer, and I got a glass of wine. I nearly emptied it in three swallows, my throat was so dry.

But as fast as I'd guzzled my wine, Roman managed to finish his beer before I emptied my glass.

I eyed the bottle he held, then looked back at him. "And I thought I was thirsty."

"Yeah." He cleared his throat and opened his mouth to say something, only to stop.

A server passed by, and we turned over our empties. I went to catch his hand, wanting to dance with him again, but when I tried to pull him to the dance floor, he pulled me in the opposite direction, toward him.

"I want to ask you something," he said in response to my questioning look.

"Oh?"

But instead of doing just that, he tugged me along behind him. We left the reception behind. I had to blink at the brightness of the lights outside the darkened ballroom, and once my eyes cleared, I looked up at Roman.

His face was…strained.

"Is everything okay?" I asked him.

"Yeah." Some of the tension faded from his features, and he reached up to cup my chin, holding me steady as he pressed his lips to mine lightly. He pulled back and held up his free hand. "No smudges, I promise."

I laughed. "The pictures are over, so if my lipstick is less than perfect, it's not a big deal."

He didn't kiss me again, though.

He took my hands, squeezing them. "Lexi, I love you."

"I love you too." I leaned in and pressed my mouth to his, ready to forget the lipstick – and the reception. I wanted to feel his mouth on mine.

He broke away before I could deepen the kiss. "I was…well…"

The nerves in his voice penetrated the sweet, warm haze of arousal, and I settled back on my feet in front of him. "What is it, Roman? Is everything okay?"

"Everything's fine. Pretty damn good, really." He crooked a grin at me, one that almost hid the nerves. "I was just…well, I think things could get *better*."

I laughed. "I'm with the guy I love at the wedding of my best friend. This is pretty spectacular."

"I know. But…"

He reached down.

My eyes widened at the sight of the little black box in his hand.

He flipped it open, and I thought my heart would just stop beating.

A diamond, set in a simple but elegant setting, sparkled up at me.

I jerked my eyes to his, and even though I knew exactly what it was, I sputtered, "W-w-what's this?"

"An engagement ring." He took my hand, gently lifting it.

My breathing hitched as he put the ring on my third finger. It fit perfectly. As perfectly as we had fit into each other's lives.

"Lexi…will you marry me?

I threw my arms around his neck, and my lipstick didn't stand a chance as I pressed my mouth to his. I was laughing and crying as I answered him.

As soon as I said, "Yes," Roman swept me up into his arms, swinging me around.

I was breathless by the time he put me back on my feet.

Breathless, and happier than I'd ever been.

"Yes," I said again. "You bet your ass I'll marry you."

THE END

Thank you so much for reading. If you enjoyed *Trapped with the Woodsman*, you'll LOVE the Hunter Brothers. CLICK HERE to check out the complete Box Set of all four brothers.

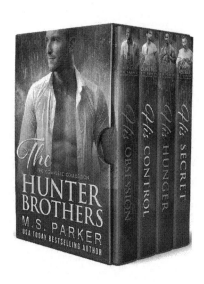

ABOUT THE AUTHOR

M. S. Parker is a USA Today Bestselling author and the author of over fifty spicy romance series and novels.

Living part-time in Las Vegas, part-time on Maui, she enjoys sitting by the pool with her laptop writing her next spicy romance.

Growing up all she wanted to be was a dancer, actor and author. So far only the latter has come true but M. S. Parker hasn't retired her dancing shoes just yet. She is still waiting for the call to appear on Dancing With The Stars.

When M. S. isn't writing, she can usually be found reading— oops, scratch that! She is always writing.

For more information:
www.msparker.com
msparkerbooks@gmail.com

ACKNOWLEDGMENTS

First, I would like to thank all of my readers. Without you, my books would not exist. I truly appreciate each and every one of you.

A big THANK YOU goes out to all the Facebook fans, street team, beta readers, and advanced reviewers. You are a HUGE part of the success of all my series.

Also thank you to my editor Lynette and my wonderful cover designer, Sinisa. You make my ideas and writing look so good.

Made in the USA
Columbia, SC
01 February 2023

11364956R00167